She took a step, but then stumbled again.

And this time she fell into his arms. Except it was more than a fall. She was so weak, she didn't hit him with a thud. She melted against him.

Not good.

Because their arms went around each other. Their bodies met. And she looked up at him. At the same moment he looked down at her.

Everything seemed to freeze.

In fact, lots of weird things happened. The memories came. Not those of the attack—something that should have been occupying his thoughts—but other memories. Those that involved kisses.

And more than kisses.

USA TODAY Bestselling Author

DELORES FOSSEN

OUTLAW LAWMAN

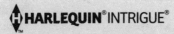
HARLEQUIN® INTRIGUE®

Recycling programs
for this product may
not exist in your area.

ISBN-13: 978-0-373-69698-7

OUTLAW LAWMAN

Printed in U.S.A.

ABOUT THE AUTHOR

Imagine a family tree that includes Texas cowboys, Choctaw and Cherokee Indians, a Louisiana pirate and a Scottish rebel who battled side by side with William Wallace. With ancestors like that, it's easy to understand why *USA TODAY* bestselling author and former air force captain Delores Fossen feels as if she were genetically predisposed to writing romances. Along the way to fulfilling her DNA destiny, Delores married an air force top gun who just happens to be of Viking descent. With all those romantic bases covered, she doesn't have to look too far for inspiration.

Books by Delores Fossen

CAST OF CHARACTERS

Marshal Harlan McKinney—Accused of a crime he didn't commit, he finds himself on the wrong side of the law and on the run with his former flame, Caitlyn, who has a killer on her trail.

Caitlyn Barnes—An investigative reporter caught in a deadly game, with old secrets and a renewed attraction for Harlan, the very lawman she's been investigating— and can't resist.

Jay Farris—He has a history of stalking Caitlyn, but he claims he's innocent.

Jonah Webb—He was once the notorious headmaster at the Rocky Creek orphanage where Caitlyn and Harlan were raised. Someone is trying to cover up the details of his murder, and that cover-up might be why Harlan and Caitlyn are in danger now.

Devin Mathis—His fiancée died in a suspicious car accident, but it could be connected to Rocky Creek and the secrets buried there sixteen years ago.

Sherry Summers—Raised at Rocky Creek with Harlan and Caitlyn, she's now missing, and her disappearance could be critical to clearing Harlan's name.

Curtis Newell—Sherry's business partner who seems desperate to find Sherry, but it could be all an act.

Billy Webb—Jonah Webb's troubled son, who has returned to the scene of his father's murder. But why come back now?

Chapter One

Marshal Harlan McKinney heard a soft clicking sound.

He waited, heard a second one and eased back the covers on his bed. In one smooth motion he snatched up his Glock from the nightstand and got to his feet.

Just as someone opened the back door of his house.

Harlan listened, hoping it was one of his foster brothers who sometimes crashed at his place. But no such luck. Since all of his brothers were federal marshals, they wouldn't have risked sneaking in at 2:00 a.m., knowing that he was armed and a light sleeper.

He heard the door being closed. Then footsteps. They were barely audible on the tiled floor of the kitchen, but the person seemed to be making a beeline for the hall that led to his bedroom and home office.

There was no time for him to pull on his jeans or boots. It was bad enough that he had an intruder, but now he'd have to bring down this person while he was wearing only boxers.

Harlan ducked behind his bedroom doorjamb and kept watch. There were no lights on in the house, but there was enough moonlight seeping through the windows that he could see the shadow that appeared on the wall.

Just a few feet away.

He didn't move. Didn't make a sound. He wanted to see if the person was armed, but he couldn't tell.

"Put your hands in the air," Harlan growled, his voice shooting through the silence.

The intruder gasped and turned as if to bolt. Harlan wasn't going to let that happen. He darn well intended to find out who was brassy or stupid enough to break into a lawman's house in the dead of night. He lunged toward the person, slamming him back against the wall.

Except it wasn't a *him*.

It didn't take long for Harlan to figure that out, because his chest landed against her breasts.

"It's me," the woman said, her breathing heavy.

Harlan instantly recognized that voice, and he reached behind him and slapped on the hall light.

Caitlyn Barnes.

It had been a few years since he'd seen her, but there was no mistaking that face.

Or that body.

Harlan had firsthand knowledge of her breasts—bare, at that—pressing against him. And while that was a pretty good memory made years ago, there weren't too many recent good memories when it came to the woman herself.

He stepped back, met her wide blue eyes. He caught just a glimpse of panic in them before she lifted her chin defiantly. He knew she was trying to look a whole lot more confident than she was. That's because he was six-three, a good eight inches taller than she was, and he outsized her by at least eighty pounds. He was a big guy, and no one had ever accused him of looking too friendly.

Plus, there was the part about him having a Glock aimed at her pretty little head.

"Most visitors just knock, even the uninvited ones,"

he snarled, easing the Glock back to his side. However, Harlan didn't ease up on the glare.

She made a sarcastic sound of agreement, huffed and put her left palm on his chest to push him back. "I didn't think you'd be here."

Well, that wasn't much of an explanation for breaking and entering or for driving all the way out to his family's ranch. The place wasn't exactly on the beaten path and was a good fifteen miles from the town of Maverick Springs, where he worked. Much too far out of the way for a friendly spur-of-the-moment visit, and Harlan let her know that with the hard look he gave her.

Caitlyn stared back, and then her gaze drifted lower. To his chest. Then lower. To his boxers. Since it wasn't anything she hadn't seen before, and because he was still waiting on that explanation, Harlan didn't budge.

But he felt that old kick of desire.

Hard not to feel it, since they'd been lovers. Well, one-time lovers anyway when they were teenagers. But once was enough. Stuff like that created bonds that weren't worth a thimbleful of spit.

Unless…

The heat was still there. Much to Harlan's disgust, it was. Probably because Caitlyn and he had spent way too much of their teens driving each other hot and crazy. He didn't intend to let it cloud his head.

For Pete's sake, the woman had broken into his home.

Just as he would have done to any other criminal caught in the act, he took her by the arm, turned her and put her face-first against the wall. Another gasp, and she tried to fight him off, but he grabbed the Colt she had tucked in the back waist of her jeans.

So not only had this blast from his past broken into his house, she'd come armed.

Harlan turned her back around and dangled her gun in front of her. "Last I heard you were a reporter," he said.

"Still am." She managed to hold her glare a moment longer before she lost the staring match and glanced away. "I came because I needed answers."

Again, no explanation for the gun or her presence, but Harlan made a circling motion with the Colt so she'd continue.

Her blue eyes snapped back to his. "Do you want me dead?"

Now, that wasn't a question he'd expected. "No," Harlan answered, and he stretched out the word a bit. "Is there a reason I'd want you dead?"

"You might think there is."

Another puzzling answer, and Harlan was getting tired of them. He wasn't a patient man, even on good days, and this didn't qualify as good in any way, fashion or form.

"A Texas Ranger came to visit me," Caitlyn said.

His heart slammed against his chest, and things became a lot clearer. "About Kirby?"

But it wasn't really a question. The Rangers were indeed investigating the sixteen-year-old murder of Jonah Webb, the SOB headmaster of the pigsty of an orphanage where Harlan and his five foster brothers had been raised.

Caitlyn, too.

Several months ago the Rangers had identified the headmaster's killer, Webb's own wife. Webb had been physically abusive, and she'd killed him during one of his beatings. But there'd been an accomplice. Neither Harlan nor any of his foster brothers had been ruled out as suspects, but the Rangers no doubt had their foster father, Kirby Granger, at the top of their list. Kirby had motive, too.

Six of them.

Because that was how many kids he'd saved from the orphanage—Harlan and the five other boys who'd become his brothers. But Kirby hadn't saved them until after Webb had been murdered.

"What'd you say to this Ranger?" Harlan asked. And it better not have been anything incriminating.

"I told him there was nothing to tell." Caitlyn paused, pushed her choppy blond hair from her face. "But he didn't believe me. He thought I was covering for one of you—even though I told him I haven't seen you or any of your foster family since we left the Rocky Creek facility after it was shut down."

That part was true. Caitlyn had been sent to another children's home, and Harlan and his foster brothers had left with Kirby. Harlan had written her, for a while anyway, and then they'd lost touch.

Until now.

Of course, he wasn't ignorant of what had happened to her. Nope. Caitlyn had become a high-profile investigative journalist. Heck, he'd even seen her on TV a couple of times while reporting stories. But then she'd practically disappeared. Why, he didn't know, and he hadn't given it much thought. Until now.

"I don't want you dead," Harlan clarified. "But I also don't want you saying anything that might get Kirby arrested. He's sick. Going through cancer treatments. And I won't have you or anyone else making his life harder than it already is. Got that?"

She nodded. "And that's why I thought you might want me out of the picture, to make sure I wouldn't implicate Kirby in Webb's murder."

Harlan didn't roll his eyes, but it was close. He tapped the top of his boxers. "Normally I wear a badge there, and I took an oath to uphold the law—"

"An oath you'd break in a heartbeat to protect Kirby," Caitlyn interrupted.

Harlan shook his head. "I can't argue with that. But murder? Really?"

"There's no love lost between us," she reminded him.

Yeah, thanks to her renegade brand of journalism that had trashed the marshals and others in law enforcement. Heck, a couple of times she'd revealed names on investigations that had come under fire, including Harlan himself. So she was right—no love lost. Still, something about this didn't make sense.

"If you thought I was out to kill you, then why come to my house?" he demanded.

"As I said, because I didn't think you'd be here." She cursed under her breath. "I wanted to search the place, to see if there was any evidence."

"Sheez. Evidence of what?"

"That you hired someone to come after me."

Harlan tried to hold on to his temper, but this was a very frustrating and confusing conversation. "Start from the beginning," he insisted.

Her gaze dropped to his boxers again. "Get dressed. Your file is in my car."

He didn't budge. "My *file?*"

"Yes, with a sworn statement from a criminal informant that you paid him to scare me, 'or worse.'"

Now it was Harlan's turn to curse, and he didn't keep it under his breath. "I've hired no one. And I want to see this file."

Another glance at his boxers. "Then I suggest you put on your jeans, because I'm parked at the end of the road."

Of course. A good quarter of a mile away. Harlan didn't mind the walk, but his mood was getting more ornery with each passing second.

Why the heck would Caitlyn think of him as a killer?

Harlan turned to go into his bedroom but decided he wasn't going to take any chances where she was concerned. He latched on to her wrist, pulled her into the bedroom with him and shut the door.

"How'd you know I lived here?" He put both her gun and his on the dresser while he pulled on his jeans.

"Research." She glanced around. Not much to see, though. A bed, dresser and nightstand. The entire house was the same—a no-frills man cave, exactly the way Harlan liked it.

"The place used to belong to Kirby's father," she remarked, probably to let him know that she had indeed done her research. "And the main ranch house where Kirby and the others live is about a mile that way." Caitlyn tipped her head in the opposite direction from where she'd said her car was parked.

"My brother Dallas doesn't live there," he disagreed, just to show her that her research sucked. And it did. Because there was no way she had any real proof that he'd hired someone to kill her.

She nodded and didn't look away when he zipped his jeans. "Because Dallas married Joelle, and they built a house on the property."

Joelle, a woman who'd once been Caitlyn's friend at Rocky Creek Children's Facility. He doubted his sister-in-law knew anything about this little visit, but he would ask her first chance he got.

Harlan put on his boots and a shirt and stuffed her Colt into the back waist of his jeans. "Why'd you think I wouldn't be here?" he asked, heading for the door.

"The P.I. that I hired said you were transporting a prisoner to Dallas."

He had been, but had finished early. The transport of a prisoner wasn't usually classified info, unless it was a high-risk, high-profile case. In this case, it wasn't. Still, it wouldn't have been common knowledge, and along with all the other things he wanted to know, Harlan would need to address that.

"What's the name of this P.I.?" He opened the front door and held it for her so that she'd be in front of him.

"I'd rather not say."

"I'd rather you did say," Harlan insisted. "In fact, I've got grounds to arrest you for breaking and entering. Don't add failure to cooperate to those charges."

Caitlyn whirled around and would have tumbled down the flagstone steps if Harlan hadn't caught her. "You're not going to arrest me."

"Who says? Give me the name of that P.I."

"Mazy Hinton." Her teeth were clenched so tightly that he was surprised she was able to speak. She tore herself from his grip and stomped through the yard toward the road.

Harlan didn't recognize the name, but within an hour or two, he'd know everything there was to know about this P.I., who was either incompetent, stupid or an out-and-out liar. None of those possibilities sat well with him.

He glanced up the road, spotted her car right where she said it would be, and he cursed both it and the August heat. There was a breeze, but it was muggy and still hot despite the late hour.

"What exactly did you think you'd find in my house?" he pressed.

She shook her head. "I wasn't sure. An email, maybe.

Or a paper trail to prove you hired someone. I wanted something in your own handwriting or from your personal computer."

Something she wouldn't find, because he hadn't done anything to set this crazy visit into motion. "I guess it didn't occur to you that if I was really a rogue marshal you should go to the cops?"

"Wasn't sure I could trust them." Ahead of him her steps slowed, and she wiped her forehead with the back of her hand. "I wasn't sure I could trust anyone. Like I said, someone's trying to scare me...or something."

"Considering your job, is that much of a surprise? You've riled a boatload of people, including me."

She turned, and in the moonlight he got a glimpse of her expression. Not the fake bravery she'd tried to sport in the hall. Not the emotions from their past. But something else. Something Harlan couldn't quite put his finger on.

"Some people do hate me," she said, as if choosing her words carefully. "But this isn't about that. The threatening notes had, well, personal details in them."

"Personal?" Harlan caught up with her, and even though they were still yards from her car, he stopped her. He whirled her back around to face him.

Not the brightest idea he'd ever had.

That whirl put them too darn close, and the breeze hit just right so that her scent washed over him. Through him, actually. Yeah, not a bright idea.

"Personal," Caitlyn verified. She took a deep breath. "The notes were typed, and they warned if I said anything about the investigation into Jonah Webb's murder, I'd be sorry. Your name was on them."

It didn't take Harlan long to figure out what this might be. "So? Anyone could have typed them."

"No. Not anyone." She didn't say anything for several moments. "Remember when we were together that night at Rocky Creek?"

Even though they'd had a lot of nights at that hellhole, Harlan figured he knew which one she meant.

"Jonah Webb went missing that night," she continued. "And we heard they were closing the place, that we'd all be split up and sent to other facilities. Well, except for Kirby Granger's *boys*. Kirby was getting all of you and some of the others out of there."

"He couldn't get you out," Harlan reminded her. "He couldn't locate your next of kin to get permission to request guardianship of you."

She gave that a dismissive nod and started walking again. "And that night we met down in the laundry room."

Their usual meeting place, where they'd talked, and kissed, for hours. They'd been barely sixteen then, but the making out had started a month earlier. It had escalated that night, and they'd had sex.

With a surprise ending.

Caitlyn had had one of the worst reputations at Rocky Creek, but Harlan had found out unexpectedly that she'd been a virgin.

"Remember what you said to me?" Caitlyn asked. *"Afterward,"* she clarified.

Yeah, he did. After sixteen years, he still did.

It had been Caitlyn's first time. Not his, though. He'd gotten lucky a few other times with girls who'd found him attractive. Sometimes he regretted that and had regretted even more that Caitlyn had given him something special—her virginity.

You'll always be my first, Caitlyn, he'd said to her. And in his crazy sixteen-year-old mind, that meant something, even though he'd omitted the critical word—*love*.

That was probably for the best, considering how things had turned out between them.

Caitlyn got to the car and threw open the passenger door. "Did you ever tell anyone else what you said to me that night?"

Harlan didn't have to think about that answer. "No. It's not the sort of thing a teenage boy chats about with his friends."

Caitlyn made a sound of agreement, fished her keys from the front pocket of her jeans and unlocked the glove compartment. She pulled out a manila folder and used her phone as a flashlight on the pages.

Harlan thumbed through the pages and saw that the first three were all typewritten and were just a few lines long.

Each had his name typed at the bottom.

But it was the threats that caught his attention.

Talk to the Rangers about Kirby and you'll be sorry, the first one read.

The second escalated. *Talk to the Rangers, and you'll die.*

He flipped the page, and he felt the knot tighten in his stomach.

Don't make me kill you had been typed in bold letters. And beneath it, *You'll always be my first, Caitlyn.*

"Hell." And that was all Harlan could manage to say for several seconds. "Believe me, I didn't send you these. If I'd wanted to warn you to keep quiet, I would have said it to your face."

She studied him, as if trying to decide if he was telling the truth, and then huffed. "There's more. Look at the next page."

He looked at the next page, but saw only a list of names and contact information.

"I'm sure you recognize them," Caitlyn said.

Harlan did. There were three names, including Caitlyn's. The two others were girls who'd lived in her dorm at the Rocky Creek Children's Facility.

Sherry Summers and Tiffany Brock.

"The three of us lived in the room nearest Jonah Webb's family quarters," Caitlyn supplied. "We were all questioned at length when Webb disappeared."

Harlan shook his head. "You think one of them sent you the threatening notes?"

"No. Tiffany's dead, killed in a car accident about two weeks ago near San Antonio." Caitlyn drew in a breath, blew it out slowly. "Her fiancé said before she died, she was getting threatening letters, warning her to stay quiet about the Webb investigation. Maybe the threats came from you. Maybe from one of your foster brothers or Kirby."

"Not a chance," Harlan jumped to answer. "Did those have my typed name on them, too?"

"No," she repeated. "And until I talked to her fiancé, he had no idea who might have sent them."

"How kind of you to fill in the blanks for him. I just wish you'd filled them in with a little truth and not some stupid speculation." He glanced at the other names. "What about Sherry?"

Another deep breath. "She's missing—for nearly three weeks now. I'm the only one left on the list, and earlier tonight I found this on my car windshield." Caitlyn turned to the next page.

It was two typewritten lines. Just a handful of words, but they caused Harlan's heart to slam against his chest.

Hell, what was going on?

Time's up, Caitlyn. Tomorrow you die.

Chapter Two

Time's up, Caitlyn. Tomorrow you die.

Caitlyn had read the latest threat so many times that she didn't need to look at it again. It was branded into her memory now, but Harlan kept his attention fixed on it for several long moments.

"I got that before midnight, which means tomorrow is already here," she added, though he no doubt had figured that out. Now what Caitlyn had to figure out was if Harlan had anything to do with it.

Judging from his reaction, the answer was no. But there was still the likelihood that someone very close to him was responsible.

He cursed and scanned the area as an experienced marshal would do to make sure they were safe. A moment later Harlan held up the note for her.

"You didn't report this to the local cops?" he demanded.

Caitlyn huffed. "If I couldn't trust you, how could I trust them?"

He cursed again. "Hell's bells, Caitlyn. According to you, a woman's dead. Another's missing, and the whack job behind all of this has clearly got you in his crosshairs." Harlan added a few more words of profanity. "How the devil could you think I'd do this to you?"

"Partly because of our last phone conversation." She gave him a moment to recall the call in question, but judging from his instant smirk he remembered it readily.

"You'd trashed the Marshals Service and me in one of your so-called pieces of journalism," he said. "And I told you what you could do with your *story*."

Exactly.

Caitlyn had only reported the facts of the case in question, but they had clashed with Harlan's version of events. Yet a dangerous criminal managed to escape while in custody of federal marshals, and that was what had happened.

Too bad it'd been on Harlan's watch.

She'd felt duty bound to report it and equally duty bound to do a follow-up piece when Harlan had been cleared of any wrongdoing. However, the follow-up hadn't soothed Harlan much.

"That phone conversation wasn't a threat," he insisted. "I was riled because you didn't wait for the whole truth before you got on TV and blabbed about it."

"It wasn't just that conversation." Caitlyn tapped the pages to remind him of something else, and in doing so her hand brushed against his. The jolt was instant.

She silently cursed it.

How could she possibly still be attracted to Harlan?

She wasn't a starry-eyed teenager anymore. She was thirty-two. Yet her hormones were zinging with just a simple touch. She blamed that on his hot cowboy looks. That black hair. Those gray eyes. Oh, and those jeans. No one should look that good in such basic clothing.

Well, it ended now. She couldn't be one of those women attracted to dangerous men.

Or potentially dangerous anyway.

Her obsession with bad boys was over, even if once she'd been proud of her own bad-girl reputation.

"It wasn't just that conversation," Caitlyn repeated after she cleared her throat. "There's the part about what you said to me that night in the laundry room at Rocky Creek. We're the only two people who knew about that." She paused. "Weren't we?"

"I thought we were." He groaned. "But obviously not. Unless you told someone."

"No." And she couldn't answer it quickly enough. "Before you ask, I didn't keep a diary. I said nothing about it in a down-memory-lane blog post. Didn't mention it in a drunken stupor either."

But yes, Caitlyn had gone through all those possibilities before she'd decided it was Harlan.

Or someone Harlan knew well.

"Maybe one of your foster brothers overheard us?" she suggested.

"And wrote the threats sixteen years later?" he finished for her, after he glared at her. "Not a chance."

"Harlan, none of you is a bloomin' Boy Scout. Kirby and all of you have reputations for bending justice now and then."

"Never justice, just the law. Something you know all about." He stared at her, practically daring her to disagree. She couldn't, especially since she'd just broken into his house.

Caitlyn did know the difference between the law and justice, but at the moment she would settle for just knowing the truth.

"How about Kirby, then?" Caitlyn tried for a slightly different angle. "Maybe he wrote the threats to keep me from talking to the Rangers?"

"No way. He's too sick. And besides, he'd rather implicate himself than me or the others."

Yes, that was exactly what she'd thought. Kirby wouldn't sell out any of them. And if Harlan had wanted to threaten her, he wouldn't have used typed notes with his name at the bottom. Still, she'd had to rule him out because of that one intimate line added to the threat.

Harlan looked at the third threat again. "The wording is exact, so it means someone overheard us. And watched us."

Caitlyn had already considered that possibility, but hearing it confirmed made her a little queasy.

Mercy.

She'd been butt naked. Harlan, too. And someone had perhaps not only watched them have sex, they'd also remembered verbatim what Harlan had said to her.

Now it was her turn to curse. "This would have been a lot easier if you'd written the notes."

He gave her a look, as if she'd sprouted a third eyeball or something.

"Easier because I'd know who was behind this," she clarified.

"Maybe, but it's obvious that someone's trying to set me up. Someone who would have been at Rocky Creek that night." Harlan looked around again. That quick, edgy sweep of the road and the pasture on both sides. "Come on. If this nut job is planning to try to kill you today, you shouldn't be out in the open like this."

That reminder unnerved her even further. She felt as if she was walking barefoot on razor blades. But she wasn't stupid, and she had taken precautions.

"That's why I brought the gun. And besides, no one followed me," she insisted.

"No one that you saw," Harlan growled. He tucked

the folder under his arm, shut her car door and took her by the shoulder again.

Caitlyn wanted to argue with that. Heck, at this point she wanted to argue with anything and anybody. She was exhausted, scared, and she'd been forced to come to the last man on earth who wanted to see her.

"Let's go back to my house so I can check some things on the computer," he added, and he got her moving in that direction. "Other than the threatening notes, has anything else happened?"

"A while back. But that had nothing to do with this."

He smirked at her again. "You got more than one person threatening you?"

"Lots of people threaten me." Caitlyn returned the smirk. "I don't exactly make a lot of friends in my job."

"That's not hard to believe," Harlan mumbled. "Anyone specific?"

She lifted her shoulder. "I had a stalker named Jay Farris. He'd leave me marriage proposals stuffed into bouquets of roses. When I turned him down, the roses became bunches of dead rats and death threats."

That required a deep breath. Caitlyn still had nightmares about him. Always would.

"The rats escalated to an attempt to strangle me one night after he'd seen me on a date with another man," she explained, not easily. Nothing was easy when it came to talking about Farris. "He wanted to kill me to prove how much he loved me."

"A real charmer, huh?" But there seemed to be more anger than sarcasm in his voice. "What happened to him?"

"He was diagnosed as a paranoid schizophrenic and placed in a mental institution. Haven't heard from him in nearly a year."

But what she left out was that Farris still had mentally haunted her all these months later. Haunted her to the point that she'd moved five times and had rarely gone into the office. She'd done most of her work from home.

"You're sure you haven't heard from Farris?" Harlan asked. "He could have sent you those notes."

Caitlyn shook her head. "No way would he have known what you said to me that night. He's seven years younger than we are, and that would have made him only nine when we were together. There weren't any kids that young in Rocky Creek."

Besides, she would have recognized an all-grown-up Farris if he'd been a fellow Rocky Creek resident. Those hard times had created bonds. Not necessarily good ones. But Caitlyn had no trouble remembering each face.

Including those of the dead and missing women.

They'd been her friends. One, Tiffany, had been her bunk mate. They'd shared every secret but one—Caitlyn hadn't told Tiff about losing her virginity to Harlan. No time for that, since both Tiff and she had been removed from Rocky Creek the following day and sent to different facilities. Caitlyn to Austin and Tiffany to San Antonio.

"Maybe Farris wasn't at Rocky Creek," Harlan said a moment later. "But he could have found out from the person who did see and hear us."

True. And despite the balmy night, that sent a chill through her.

Judas priest.

Farris had money from his family's hugely successful computer software business and could have hired someone to do his dirty work.

But why would Farris tell her not to talk to the Rangers?

He wouldn't.

Farris had no connection to what had gone on at Rocky Creek and Jonah Webb. At least, she was reasonably sure of that, but Caitlyn made a mental note to do more checking.

"How did you find out about Tiffany's car accident and that Sherry was missing?" Harlan did another of those glances around, and it made her consider running to his house. Thankfully, it wasn't far away, and she could see the light he'd left on in the hall.

"Tiff's fiancé called to let me know about her death. He asked me to get in touch with anyone from Rocky Creek who might want to know. I haven't stayed in touch with anyone, but I tried to track down Sherry. She runs an investment firm in Houston, and her business partner, Curtis Newell, said she left without giving him any notice."

"Maybe Sherry doesn't want to be found." Harlan shrugged. "Could be she just needs some downtime."

Caitlyn had already considered that and more. "None of her friends knows where she is. *None.* That's suspicious to me, and there doesn't appear to be any crisis going on in her life that would make her disappear. Also, she didn't actually tell anyone in person that she was leaving."

Harlan made a *hmm* sound to indicate he was thinking about that. "I'll call around, see what I can find. It could turn out to be nothing." He led her through the yard and to the porch. "Still, it's suspicious, especially when you consider everything else."

Harlan opened the front door, but then stopped and turned to face her. "For the record, if anything like this happens again, don't assume I'm out to kill you. And don't break into my house—*ever.*"

The last word had hardly left his mouth when Caitlyn saw alarm go through Harlan's eyes. She shook her head, not understanding, but she didn't have time to ask what had put the alarm there.

Harlan dropped the folder, letting it slip from his arm and onto the floor, and in the same motion he spun away from her. Toward the living room.

But it was too late.

Caitlyn saw the movement behind them. Someone in the shadows. And that someone pointed a gun directly at Harlan.

But it wasn't a gun.

It was a Taser.

One hit from it, and Harlan let out a choked groan. She watched in horror as he dropped to the floor.

Caitlyn heard the scream bubble up in her throat, and she turned to grab Harlan's gun.

God. This couldn't be happening. Not again. Here she was fighting for her life, and worse. Harlan was in grave danger, too.

She didn't get a chance to grab the gun. No chance to do anything. She made it only a few steps before she felt the jolt from the Taser. It crackled through her entire body.

Just like that, she had no control. No chance to scream or get away.

Nothing.

Caitlyn couldn't even turn to see her attacker's face. But she heard the voice. It was like something from a cartoon. There was no humor in it, though, only fear that spread like ice through her veins when he whispered a warning.

"Time's up, Caitlyn."

Chapter Three

Harlan winced at the dull throbbing ache in his head. But when he opened his eyes, the glare of sunlight turned the ache into a jolt of pain that nearly knocked the breath right out of him.

No time to adjust to the light and pain, though. He had to fight back.

He had to save Caitlyn and himself.

That reminder gave him a much-needed spike of adrenaline, and he shot to a sitting position and reached for his gun.

It wasn't there.

He blinked, focusing, and glanced around for his Glock. No shoulder holster. No Glock. In fact, the only thing he was wearing was his boxers.

Hell.

What was going on?

He dragged in a few quick breaths, hoping to clear his head. It helped. The last thing he remembered was being in the doorway of his house and someone shooting him with one of those long-range projectile Tasers. Well, he wasn't in his house now.

But he didn't know where he was.

It was a motel room from the looks of it, and he was on the bed. Not alone, though. That gave him another jolt of adrenaline, and his body went into fight mode until he realized the person beside him was Caitlyn.

She was wearing only her bra and panties. Skimpy ones at that.

And she wasn't moving.

Harlan nearly shouted out her name, but then realized it wouldn't be a smart thing to do. That was because he noticed something else—his left wrist was handcuffed to her right. He certainly didn't remember that about the attack, but he was guessing Caitlyn hadn't been the one to do this.

That meant they were not alone.

"Caitlyn?" he whispered.

No response. He put his left hand to her throat and felt her pulse. Steady and strong. That was good. But other than being alive, there wasn't much else good about this.

He tried again to wake Caitlyn while he looked around to assess their *situation*. It was a bare-bones kind of room. Bed, dresser, two nightstands and a TV. No phone, though. The adjoining bathroom door was wide-open, and while he couldn't see anyone, that didn't mean someone wasn't in the shower. Or the closet.

The someone who'd cuffed them.

But in the main part of the room there were no signs of anyone but Caitlyn and him. Heck, he didn't even see their clothes. Whatever had happened, they were clearly being held captive, and that meant they needed to get out of there. Or at least find some way to defend themselves.

Harlan gave Caitlyn's arm a hard shake, and this time he got a response. A groggy moan.

"Wake up," Harlan insisted. "We have to leave now."

Easier said than done. Because of the cuffs and the tornado going on in his head, he couldn't just bolt from the bed, but he hauled Caitlyn to a sitting position, anchoring her in place so she wouldn't topple back over. Her eyes finally eased open, and as he'd done, she looked around.

"Where are we?" she mumbled at the same moment that Harlan asked, "Any idea how we got here?"

Caitlyn groaned when she looked first at what she was wearing. Or rather what she wasn't wearing—clothes. And then at the cuffs.

"What happened after I got hit with the Taser?" he asked. Harlan got to his feet, looped his arm around her waist and helped her stand.

"I don't know." She tried to put her hand against her forehead. Probably because like him, she was in pain. But the handcuffs sent Harlan's arm brushing across her breasts.

"Sorry," she mumbled. Caitlyn blew out another breath. "I saw you get hit with the Taser, and I tried to get your gun. My gun," she corrected. "You'd put it in the back waist of your jeans."

Yeah. He remembered that part. The part about falling flat on the hardwood floor, too—emphasis on the *hard*. But that was where his memories stopped. Obviously Caitlyn had been attacked second, and that meant she might recall more than he did.

"You remember anything after he got you with the Taser?" he asked.

"No." She glanced around the room again. "I certainly don't remember being brought here. Or having my clothes taken off. Did you do that?"

He shook his head and was reasonably sure he would have remembered undressing Caitlyn. Or someone else undressing her in front of him. And that could mean only one thing.

"After the Taser hit, someone must have drugged us,"

Harlan explained. It was the only thing that made sense, and yet it didn't make sense at all.

"God," Caitlyn mumbled. She jerked her uncuffed hand to her mouth and pressed her fingers there for several seconds.

Harlan didn't like that *God* one bit. "What do you remember?"

She looked at him, blinked, and along with the grogginess, he could see fear in her eyes. "The person was using one of those voice scramblers, and he said something to me." She gulped in some air. "'Time's up, Caitlyn.'"

Tears watered her eyes, and he saw the muscles in her body tense. She was terrified. With reason.

"It's okay," Harlan tried to assure her. But it was a lie. Everything was far from *okay,* and it wouldn't get even marginally better until they were in a safe place. "You're still alive, so he obviously didn't carry through on his threat."

But why not?

It was a sickening thought, but their attacker had had plenty of time and opportunity to kill them both.

With his arm still looped around her, Harlan grabbed the lamp from the nightstand, the only semi-weapon in the room, and went to the window. He stayed to the side, keeping Caitlyn behind him, and eased back the curtain.

Yeah, they were definitely in a motel, and not a high-end one either. The window and front door faced a parking lot where there were several vehicles. However, he didn't see his truck or Caitlyn's car.

"Ever heard of the Starlight Inn?" he asked, noting the large sign at the end of the parking lot.

"No." She pressed her body against him when she peered over his shoulder. "It doesn't look familiar."

Not to him either, and they sure weren't in Maverick Springs. Harlan had lived there for sixteen years since he'd left Rocky Creek, and he knew every nook and cranny of the town.

So where were they, and who'd brought them here?

"I need to check the bathroom." With Caitlyn in tow, he started in that direction. Where their captor could be hiding.

Of course, there was no reason for the person to hide, since he was calling the shots here. But Harlan hoped he was there so he could bash the moron to bits for doing whatever the hell he'd done to them.

That gave Harlan a moment's pause.

What exactly had he done to them?

He glanced at Caitlyn again, specifically at her body, running his gaze from her face to her breasts to her belly, where he spotted a tiny black ink tattoo with letters.

And then below.

There didn't appear to be anything obvious, like love bites or bruises, but they were wearing just underwear and had woken up in a bed.

"Did we…?" she asked, clearly picking up on the reason he was gawking at her body.

"No." And that, too, could be a whopper of a lie, especially if someone had given them a drug that had caused memory loss. But Harlan wasn't going to worry about that now, particularly since they had more immediate problems.

With the lamp ready as a club, he went in ahead of Caitlyn. The shower curtain was closed. Of course. No chance that any of this would be easy. Harlan readied himself and used his foot to shove back the vinyl curtain. It slithered open, the metal rings jangling on the overhead bar and sounding far more sinister than it would have under normal circumstances.

Empty.

Well, it was empty except for their clothes and shoes, which had been neatly folded and placed in the tub.

Harlan tossed the lamp aside and rifled through the garments, looking for either his or Caitlyn's gun. They weren't there. Neither were their phones or a key for the cuffs.

"What's going on?" Caitlyn asked. She grabbed her jeans and started to put them on. Not easily because of the blasted handcuffs.

Harlan put on his jeans, too. Best not to go after their captor while he was practically butt naked. "I'm not sure. But judging from what this dirt-for-brains said to you about time being up, it's all part of the threats. That could mean we're back to someone who doesn't want you talking to the Rangers or your stalker, Farris. He could have hired someone to do this, or maybe he's out of the institution."

That sort of stuff happened all the time. Inmates were released and no one bothered to tell the victims.

"No," she said while she put on her shoes. "If Farris were out, he would have just killed me. He wouldn't have drugged us and brought us here."

She was obviously basing that conclusion on his previous attack, when he'd tried to strangle her. Something that turned Harlan's stomach. But Farris could have taken a new direction in his criminal activity, so Harlan wasn't going to rule him out. No. Just the opposite.

Farris—or the person he'd hired—was at the top of his list.

Harlan tugged on his boots and looped his shirt over his arm, since there was no way he could put it on. Caitlyn, however, ripped the right side and sleeve of her top so she could cover herself. Probably for the best. Her bra and what was beneath it were just plain distracting.

Too many memories.

Harlan headed back to the front door, but he took a moment to rifle through the nightstand drawer to find something—anything—he could use to pick the lock on the handcuffs. But there wasn't a stray paper clip. That meant going outside without being able to give Farris, or whoever had done this, a full fight.

There was a local telephone directory in the bottom drawer. Not thick or big enough. While it wouldn't stop a bullet, he grabbed it and rolled it so that it formed a nightstick of sorts. Hardly his weapon of choice when they didn't know what they were up against, but maybe he could avoid a showdown until he was in a better position to kick somebody's butt for doing this to Caitlyn and him.

"Stay behind me," Harlan warned Caitlyn, and he eased open the door and looked outside.

It was early morning, maybe seven or so, and there was no one in the parking lot, but a car did go by on the street in front of the motel. It didn't stop, and Harlan didn't call out to the driver.

That was because he had a bad feeling they were being watched.

After all, why would someone go to all the trouble of using a Taser on them, drugging them and bringing them to this place only to let them easily escape?

Harlan kept close to the building and headed for the office sign at the front. Right by the road. Once inside he could call his brothers, who were no doubt wondering where the heck he was. It was a workday, and he should have already been at the marshals' office in Maverick Springs.

He and Caitlyn were still a good twenty yards from the office when a dark blue truck turned into the parking lot. But it didn't just turn. The tires squealed as the driver whipped into the lot, and Harlan automatically pulled Caitlyn to the ground in front of one of the parked cars, an older-model red four-door sedan.

The truck slowed once it was in the lot, and the driver inched around, pausing in front of each door. Maybe checking the numbers? Maybe looking for any sign of them.

Or witnesses.

That was a strong possibility, since there appeared to be other guests staying at the motel. The driver finally came to a stop in the parking spot directly in front of the room they'd just escaped from.

Harlan stayed low, pulling Caitlyn as far behind him as he could manage. He watched. And held his breath. He didn't want to fight like this. Not where Caitlyn could be in the line of fire and also in his way. He wouldn't be able to fight while handcuffed to her.

It didn't take long, just a few seconds, before the truck door flew open and the driver stepped out. A man wearing dark clothes. He kept his back to Harlan, so he couldn't see his face, and he didn't recognize the man's gait. However, he thought he might recognize the gun he held next to his right leg. It looked exactly like Harlan's standard-issue Glock.

Harlan tried to take in as many details of the man as he could, including the number of his license plate and the way he practically kicked down the door of the motel room. Whoever this guy was, he was riled to the core, and that meant there'd be no showdown between

Harlan and him. Not at this moment anyway, but once he had Caitlyn someplace safe, he was coming after this dirt wipe.

"You know that guy?" Harlan asked her.

"Hard to tell." Her breath was racing, hitting against his bare shoulder and back, and every muscle in her arm was iron hard. "But it could be Farris. We need to find out if he's out of the institution."

He would. And maybe Caitlyn would be able to confirm if it was or wasn't Farris when she got a look at his face. The trick was to let Caitlyn get that look without the guy seeing her. Harlan didn't want the man using that Glock on them.

From inside the room, Harlan heard a loud crash, as if someone had bashed something against the wall. Harlan waited with his breath held, and within seconds the man burst out of the room.

Caitlyn groaned softly, and Harlan knew why.

They couldn't see his face to determine if it was her stalker because the guy was wearing a ski mask. He jumped back into the truck and sped away. He was already a few yards past the vehicle where they were hiding when the driver of the truck slammed on his brakes.

"What's he doing?" Caitlyn asked, her voice a hoarse whisper.

Harlan didn't answer. Didn't want to make a sound, but he eased himself lower to the ground so he could watch from beneath the car.

His heart slammed against his ribs when he heard the truck door open again. And Harlan saw black combat boots when the guy stepped out. The man didn't move for what seemed to be an eternity, and it gave Harlan too much time to think of all the things that could go wrong.

"Get back in the truck," Harlan said to himself, hoping the guy would do just that.

But he didn't.

He took a step. Then another.

Oh, hell.

The armed man was walking straight toward them.

Chapter Four

It took every bit of Caitlyn's self-control—and Harlan's bruising grip on her arm—to stay in her place. Her instincts were screaming for her to bolt. To get far away from the ski-masked man who was just a few yards away and closing in fast. But running would only get her shot.

Harlan, too.

Because she hadn't missed that the man coming toward them was also armed. And angry. Everything about his body language told her he was working on a short fuse and a hot temper, and it was too much to hope that all that fury was aimed at someone other than Harlan and her.

But why?

Soon she wanted to know the answer to that, but unfortunately they might be killed before they learned why this man was after them.

Even though she tried not to make a sound, that was just about impossible with her heart and breath galloping out of control. Unlike Harlan. He was focused only on the man's movement, and he didn't show any sign of the fear Caitlyn was feeling.

She glanced around them, looking for anything she could use as a weapon. The only things within reach were a couple of small rocks, so Caitlyn scooped them up and waited. God, she wished they had a phone so she could at least call the cops.

The man stopped, and Caitlyn pulled in her breath. Held it. Waiting and praying that he would just turn around, go back to his truck and drive away.

That didn't happen.

Because her attention was nailed to him, she saw the shift of his weight to the front of his feet, and he slowly bent his knees. Lowering himself. Stooping down. And there was only one reason for him to do that.

So he could look beneath the cars.

Caitlyn tried to hold out hope that he wouldn't see them. Or that someone would see him and send him running. After all, a man in a ski mask was bound to look suspicious.

Harlan turned his head slightly to the side. "Get ready to move," he mouthed.

That caused panic to shoot through her again. Move where? There were only two places for them to go—right or left—and either way the man would see them.

Even though she'd braced herself for the man to fire, it was still a hard jolt when the blast came. In the same second, Harlan used their handcuffed connection to jerk her to the side. Away from the bullet that slammed into the ground.

The sound was deafening, and it seemed to echo through the parking lot. No way the guests would miss that, and it would certainly prompt someone to call the cops.

She hoped.

Still, it wouldn't help them now.

The sound she didn't hear was a car alarm. Caitlyn had hoped there'd be one and that the blaring noise would send the man running back to his truck. It didn't. No alarm, just the man coming for them.

Harlan didn't stay put. He shoved her behind him as far as he could. Which wasn't far. And he dragged them to the side of the vehicle.

Even over the roar in her ears, Caitlyn had no trouble hearing the man's footsteps. Definitely not light. More like stomps. Of course, she already knew he was in a rage, so it was no surprise that he was coming at them like a madman.

But why was he trying to kill them now when he'd had plenty of time to do it while they'd been unconscious inside the motel room?

Caitlyn didn't have time to consider an answer because there was another shot. This one tore through the hood of the car and came so close to them that she could swear she felt the heat and movement of the bullet.

Shoving her along, Harlan hurried to the back of the car, and he dragged her behind the beat-up old station wagon next to them. She caught just a glimpse of the shooter before another bullet came their way. This one tore off a chunk of the car's bumper.

Still no car alarm.

Harlan kept them moving. Away from the shooter and toward the motel check-in. That didn't deter the man. She could still hear his stomps, but she also heard something else.

Shouts.

Someone was yelling out to call 911, but the shots kept away anyone who might otherwise want to help. She prayed no one inside the rooms would get hurt.

Harlan pulled her to the far side of the station wagon. Still three vehicles away from the motel office. Way too far to make a run for it, and besides, if the clerk was smart, he would have already locked the door.

"Hell," she heard Harlan mumble.

And she soon realized why. The shooter wasn't just stomping now. He'd broken into a run.

Heading right for them.

Harlan levered himself up and hurled the rolled-up phone book at the guy. From the sound it made, it smacked him somewhere on the body, but she didn't see exactly where. That was because Harlan got them moving again—this time to a small car that put them one step closer to the office.

Another shot.

Then another.

The bullets tore right through the small car and slammed into the truck parked next to it. The sound was instant. A shrill blast from the truck's security alarm. But the noise did something else that Caitlyn hadn't counted on.

It drowned out their attacker's footsteps.

She had no idea where he was, but that lasted only a few seconds. She soon saw his exact location.

The man barreled around the back of the small car, and before he even came to a stop, he was already taking aim. Harlan was moving, too. Trying to get them out of the line of fire.

Caitlyn scrambled as Harlan dragged her along, but she turned and tossed the handful of rocks right at the guy.

Pay dirt.

The rocks distracted him, and his shot was off. The bullet slammed into the ground, sending a spray of sharp chunks of concrete at them. Even with the debris, Harlan managed to get them to cover behind the next vehicle.

Their attacker made a feral sound. A sort of outraged growl, but he didn't speak.

He fired another shot, but this one didn't come anywhere near close to them. Good. Maybe he was no longer in control.

Over the shrill car alarm Caitlyn heard another sound. A welcome one. Sirens. And they already sounded close.

Harlan pulled her farther down to the concrete, and for a moment she thought he'd done that because he'd gotten a glimpse of the shooter, but he peered under the vehicle.

"He's getting away."

Because of the clamor of sirens and noise, Caitlyn didn't actually hear Harlan's words, but she saw them form on his mouth. The relief was instant, but it was quickly replaced by another feeling. Major concern. If the shooter managed to escape, they might never know who he was or why he'd launched this attack.

Harlan made a quick peek over the hood of the car, and he cursed. She soon figured out why. The truck zipped past them, flying across the parking lot.

That got Harlan and her to their feet, and she prayed the cops were there, in place and ready to stop this guy.

But they weren't.

The truck bolted out of the parking lot and onto the street that fronted the motel.

Still cursing, Harlan got them moving again toward the motel office. "Keep your hands up so everyone can see them," he warned her.

Mercy. Caitlyn hadn't considered that someone might think they'd fired those shots, but in the chaos of a situation, anything could happen. They lifted their hands just as two police cruisers braked to a stop. Not in the parking lot but on the very street where the gunman had just escaped.

With their guns drawn, the cops barreled out and used their cruisers for cover. They aimed their weapons at Harlan and her.

"I'm Marshal Harlan McKinney," he shouted over the alarm. "You need to go after the driver of a blue truck." And he rattled off the license plate.

The cops didn't move, and she couldn't blame them. Harlan and she were handcuffed together, disheveled and probably didn't look like victims of a kidnapping, even if that was exactly what they were.

Now Caitlyn cursed. It would take precious minutes, maybe longer, for the cops to sort all of this out, and the shooter could be long gone by then.

The door to the motel office opened just a fraction, and a lanky man poked his head out a few inches. "The guy that drove out of here fired shots at them," he confirmed.

But that still didn't get the cops moving. The four officers said something to each other. Something she couldn't catch because of the alarms, but Harlan started lowering himself to his knees. Caitlyn did the same, and soon she found herself facedown on the concrete.

Finally the cops came out from cover and made their way toward them. Also, the alarm stopped so she could actually hear what they were saying.

"Marshal McKinney?" one of the uniforms called out.

"Yeah," Harlan verified. "There's probably a missing persons report on me."

"There is," the cop verified. He looked at his phone and then at Harlan, probably comparing a photo to his face.

She hadn't even considered that Harlan's brothers

would be looking for him and would have alerted the authorities, but Caitlyn was thankful they had.

"No missing report on you," the cop said to her. "But you look familiar. Are you that reporter?"

She settled for mumbling a yes, since she and the cops were rarely in the same corner. This was one exception, though. She was thankful beyond words to have been rescued.

The cop reached down and helped them back to their feet, but Harlan didn't stay put. He immediately started toward the cruisers.

"We need to go in pursuit now," Harlan insisted, and it sounded like an order. "And get us out of these damn cuffs."

The cop didn't argue, and as they approached the other officers, she heard one of them phoning in the shooter's license plate. Maybe they'd get lucky and catch him, but Caitlyn's heart dropped when she saw they were on an access road. The ramp to the interstate was literally just yards away.

One look at Harlan, and she saw the frustration and anger in his eyes, too.

"What happened to you two?" the lanky officer asked them. His name tag identified him as Sergeant Eric Tinsley.

Harlan threw open the side door of the cruiser and jumped in, pulling her practically into his lap, since there wasn't much room in the passenger seat.

"I can't let you do this," Tinsley said.

Harlan met the cop's gaze. "This guy kidnapped us and tried to kill us. He's not getting away."

And while Harlan's tone left no room for doubt about that, they both knew the shooter was doing just that—getting away.

"When the motel clerk called 911, he gave a description of the vehicle," Tinsley said. "Law enforcement will be on the lookout for it."

"That's not enough," Harlan insisted. "I need to find this guy."

Tinsley looked around as if figuring out what to do, but then he tipped his head to the backseat of the cruiser. "Get in and buckle up so my partner can ride with us. Can't do this without backup, and you're not exactly in any position to assist."

Harlan made an even more frustrated sound of agreement and got her moving into the backseat. There was a metal mesh divider between the front and back. Clearly for prisoner transport, but she didn't care about that. Caitlyn only wanted to go after the shooter.

Thankfully, that didn't take long.

Tinsley's partner tossed Harlan a key that he took from the glove compartment, and he jumped in. "It's a universal key," he explained as they sped away from the motel.

Harlan didn't waste any time unlocking the cuffs, and Caitlyn's hand dropped like a stone. The muscles in her hand and arm were knotted. Her head was still pounding, too, but those were minor things. At the moment no one was shooting at them, and maybe they could get a lot of answers as to why this had happened, if they could just catch up with that blue truck.

A truck she didn't see.

Tinsley drove up the ramp and onto the interstate, and while there were a few other trucks on the road, the blue one was nowhere in sight.

Mercy.

They had to find him.

"Who's this shooter?" Tinsley asked.

Harlan didn't have time to answer because Tinsley's phone rang. A few moments later he hung up and shook his head. "You're sure that was the right license plate for the blue truck?"

"Positive." Harlan didn't look at the man when he answered. He was literally on the edge of the seat, checking out the traffic while he shoved his arm through the sleeve of his shirt.

"Then it's bogus," Tinsley informed them.

She didn't know who groaned louder—Harlan or her. Now there was no way to know who owned the vehicle unless they found it, and with each passing mile, her hopes were getting lower and lower in that department.

"He's not working alone," Harlan said, glancing first at her and then briefly meeting Tinsley's gaze in the rearview mirror. "Someone hit us with a Taser, drugged us and put us in that motel room."

"You saw more than one person?" Tinsley asked.

"No, but if the shooter had been the one to put us there, he wouldn't have had to look for the room."

Caitlyn thought back to those terrifying moments before the shooting. The man hadn't gone directly to the room, and he'd spent some time inside looking around. He probably wouldn't have had to do that if he'd known all along they were there.

That tightened the knot in her stomach.

God, how many were in on this?

"One man probably couldn't have carried me," Harlan muttered, as if he knew exactly what she was thinking.

Yeah. Harlan was a big guy, and that meant there had probably been at least two who'd carried them from his house and to the motel. Caitlyn didn't want to think of what else those men had done, but she was positive she hadn't been raped. That was something, at least. A *big* something.

"This has to be connected to Rocky Creek," she said to Harlan. All those threats couldn't be coincidence.

But then she had to shake her head.

Time's up, Caitlyn. Tomorrow you die. That had been the last threat she'd received, and it hadn't happened. The guy with the Taser hadn't killed her, though he would have had ample opportunity to do just that. Plus, it would have been a heck of a lot easier than drugging them and dragging them to that motel.

Almost as if they'd been bait.

Or something.

"What's the date?" she asked.

The officers seemed surprised, but Tinsley checked his watch. "The fourteenth."

"It's still *tomorrow*," Harlan verified. "And I'm pretty sure the shooter was supposed to make that threat come true."

Yes. And he nearly had. She'd lost count of how many shots he'd fired, but any one of them could have hit Harlan and her.

"He wasn't an expert shot," Harlan continued. "And it was personal."

Caitlyn couldn't argue with either of those points. "That leads us back to Farris."

She was about to ask for a phone so she could make some calls to find out if Farris was indeed still in the institution, but she stopped when she spotted the truck just ahead. Not speeding away. Not even on the interstate.

But rather at a standstill in the emergency lane.

"That's it," Harlan told the officers.

Tinsley turned on the lights and siren, called for backup and eased to a stop behind the truck. Caitlyn

tried to look inside the vehicle, but Harlan didn't give
her a chance. He caught the back of her neck and pushed
her down on the seat.

"Stay put," Harlan insisted.

Tinsley looked back at Harlan as if he might tell him
the same thing, but he didn't stop Harlan from getting
out with him and his partner. Both cops drew their weapons, and they stayed behind the cover of their doors while
they kept their attention fastened on the truck.

Caitlyn lifted her head just a little so she could look,
too, but the back window on the truck had a heavy tint,
and she couldn't see inside the truck cab.

Tinsley called out for the driver to exit the vehicle. No
response, though. Ditto for his second attempt.

The seconds dragged by, and even though Caitlyn
tried to keep her heartbeat and breathing steady, she
failed big-time. She'd known she was in danger before
she even went to Harlan's place, but she hadn't considered that she could be bringing the danger to him.

He could be killed.

Right here, if the gunman started shooting.

Even though there was bad blood between them, the
last thing she wanted was him to be hurt. Or involved
in this. But then she rethought that, too.

Harlan was involved.

One of the threats had even mentioned what he'd said
to her that night they'd had sex. So maybe the person
behind all of this had written that knowing it would
make her suspect Harlan. Knowing that she would go
running to him.

If so, this was all her fault.

Her breath stalled again when the cops began to inch
toward the truck door, and Harlan stayed right with them
despite the fact that he wasn't armed. Each step they

took put her heart higher in her throat, but she could only sit there, watch and pray that this was all about to end. If they had the shooter, then they would know who was behind this.

And why.

Tinsley approached the driver's side. His partner, the other. But Harlan moved even closer to Tinsley when the officer peered into the window. He said something to Harlan. Something she couldn't hear, but Caitlyn didn't need to hear the words to see the frustration in Tinsley's body language.

It was Harlan who threw open the driver's door, and again she didn't need to hear what he said to know he was cursing a blue streak. That was the last straw.

Nothing could have held Caitlyn back at that point.

She bolted from the cruiser to see what had caused the profanity and frustration. And she soon saw.

The truck was empty.

She looked back to the interstate, hoping she'd catch a glimpse of the shooter—maybe on foot, maybe driving away in another vehicle. It was possible he was doing just that, but if so, he was nowhere in sight.

"He left something," Harlan said.

Caitlyn followed his gaze and soon saw what had captured Harlan's attention. A folded piece of paper was on the steering wheel.

"I want it processed for prints." But Harlan didn't touch it. No doubt because he didn't want to disturb any evidence that the shooter might have left, not just on the paper but in the truck itself.

"Something's written on it," Tinsley pointed out.

"Yeah." Harlan shook his head, repeated it. "It's a message," he said, looking at Caitlyn. "For you."

Chapter Five

Harlan cursed the bad phone reception at the Maverick Springs Hospital, and everything else he could think of.

There was a lot on that particular list.

He could make out only half of what his brother Slade Becker was saying, but even so, Harlan wasn't hearing anything good.

His other brother Declan had brought Harlan his phone from the house because it had all his contact numbers, but what he needed was to hear some good news.

According to Slade, there was no sign of the shooter and no security cameras at the motel in Cross Creek where he and Caitlyn had been taken, cuffed and left for a killer to finish them off. If the crappy news had ended there, it might not have been so bad.

But it didn't.

Sergeant Tinsley had added to the growing heap of *bad* by telling Harlan that there didn't appear to be any prints or traces in either the truck or on the note the SOB had left with Caitlyn's name scrawled on the folded sheet of paper. A note with just a handful of words.

This isn't over. You're a dead woman.

Harlan wanted to disagree with that threat, but he couldn't. As long as the shooter and his accomplice were out there, this was far from over for Caitlyn. And as for the dead part—well, that's what he had to stop from happening.

"What about any info on Jay Farris?" Harlan asked his brother.

"Still trying. He was transferred to a private facility about a month ago—" And the rest was static gibberish, but Harlan thought Slade said something about the facility not giving them access to records without a court order. "You've got to call the Ranger back, Harlan."

Now, that part came through loud and clear.

Figures.

It was the one thing in this conversation that he didn't want relayed, because the Ranger in question was none other than Griffin Morris, who'd been assigned to investigate Jonah Webb's murder. If Harlan had thought for one second that Morris had any info about this incident, he'd be on the phone to him, but no. Morris wanted to question Harlan as a possible suspect—accessory to Webb's murder.

Harlan didn't have time for that.

The door to the examining room opened finally, and Harlan told Slade that he would call him back. Right now he needed to make sure Caitlyn was all right, and judging from the glimpse that Harlan got of her face from over the doctor's shoulder, she wasn't. She was shades too pale and looked ready to collapse.

Dr. Cheryl Landry stopped in the doorway and met Harlan's gaze. "She'll be okay. Your turn now. Want to go into the examining room next door so I can give you a checkup?"

"It can wait." Yet something else he didn't have time for—and besides, he'd already done the important part. He'd had the lab draw a blood sample to see if they could identify what had been used to drug him.

The doctor frowned, but she didn't look surprised. Probably because she'd been stitching up Harlan and his brothers for the better part of a decade. She knew cooperation wasn't their strong suit.

"At least get some rest," the doctor grumbled. "And that goes for both of you. I'll call as soon as I have the lab results from the tox screens." She walked away, still mumbling and scribbling something on a chart.

Caitlyn didn't get up from the examining table. Practically limp, she sat there wearing green scrubs that were identical to Harlan's. One of the first things on his to-do list was to get them a change of clothes, since theirs had been bagged for processing. He doubted there'd be any usable trace evidence on them, but their luck might change.

He sure as heck hoped so anyway.

Harlan walked closer, easing the door shut behind him so he could ask her a question that he wasn't sure how to ask. He played with the words in his head, but Caitlyn beat him to it.

"I wasn't sexually assaulted," she volunteered. "No signs of recent sex, consensual or otherwise."

Harlan was relieved but not surprised. Well, not surprised except for the recent-sex part. With Caitlyn's looks, he figured she must have a current lover, but maybe Farris had destroyed that part of her life, too.

Thankfully, he'd seen no indications on her body of a violent attack, and he'd gotten an up-close-and-personal look at it, since she'd been wearing only panties and a bra in bed. Besides, if they'd had sex he would have remembered.

Even drugs wouldn't have blocked that out.

Hell, bad blood and sixteen years hadn't been able to make him forget having sex with her.

"I'm guessing there are no breaks in the investigation," she mumbled, pushing her hair away from her face.

Harlan shook his head and caught her arm when she practically stumbled off the table. "There's some red tape involved in getting more info about Farris at the private facility where he was transferred. Did you know he'd been moved?"

"No." She gave a weary sigh and looked up at him with those equally weary blue eyes. "I went in the wrong direction on this. All those threats seemed to point to you."

And he wasn't too happy that she'd jumped to believe the worst about him. But then he mentally shrugged. She'd probably thought the worst because in their last conversation they'd been at each other's throats.

He'd blasted her six ways to Sunday over that article she'd written about him.

"We can go back to my place and wait," he insisted. "You need to get some rest and something to eat. And we can make a few calls to try to speed up all the wheels that are turning right now."

He'd also have to put some time in at the office, but the adrenaline crash was getting to him, too.

"Is my car still at your house?" she asked.

"Yeah." It was one of the things he'd managed to hear Slade confirm. Her car was there, and there'd been no damage to the place. "But you're not driving anywhere. It's not safe, Caitlyn."

He braced himself for a big argument. Caitlyn was even more pigheaded than he was, but it had to be a sign of exhaustion when she only shrugged. "I just want to catch this bastard."

Harlan was right there with her. Literally. She took a step but then stumbled again. And this time she fell into his arms. Except it was more than a fall. She was so weak, she didn't hit him with a thud. She melted against him.

Not good.

Because their arms went around each other. Their bodies met. And she looked up at him. At the same moment he looked down at her.

Everything seemed to freeze.

In fact, lots of weird things happened. The memories came. Not those of the attack—something that should have been occupying his thoughts—but other memories. Those that involved kisses.

And more than kisses.

The corner of her mouth lifted, and that half smile seemed as wobbly as the rest of her. She gave his arm a pat, grazing his chest in the process. The rest of her did a little grazing, too. But she didn't move away.

Neither did Harlan.

Oh, man. He didn't need this now. Not ever. The memories were bad enough, but now his asinine body was starting to act as if it was about to get lucky.

It wasn't.

And Harlan repeated that to himself.

"Even hate can't cool *that* down," Caitlyn mumbled. With that shocker of a remark, she brushed her mouth over his, opened the door and headed out.

Harlan was right behind her, but it took him a moment to get his tongue untangled over that blasted half kiss. Man, something that wussy shouldn't have packed such a wallop.

"I don't hate you," he clarified, choosing to deal with the easier part of that shocker. He didn't intend to touch the other with a ten-foot pole. "I hated what you did. I don't like it when people screw around with my badge and career."

"That article was my career," she countered. "If I hadn't written it, someone else would have."

That was probably true, but this wasn't a reasoning kind of thing here. Her article had painted him and the Marshals Service in a bad light, and he'd caught a boatload of flak over it. Flak he'd aimed right back at her when he'd called her.

"I'm not a jerk," she added, "but sometimes I have to make decisions I don't want to make." Caitlyn stopped and looked out when they reached the door.

Just as Harlan did. He didn't see anyone ready to gun them down, but his brother Declan was waiting, leaning against his truck, which was parked next to one of the standard-issue cars that Harlan had used to drive them from headquarters to the hospital.

"Declan," Caitlyn said, and she hurried to him and pulled him into her arms for a hug.

Harlan wasn't jealous of his little brother, but it was a little unnerving to see Caitlyn nestled there as if it were the most natural place on earth for her to be.

Declan smiled and lifted a strand of her hair. "Last time I saw you, it was pink, and you had a nose ring."

She returned the smile. "Last time I saw you, you weren't taller than me."

Declan put his mouth to her ear, whispered something. When he was done, Caitlyn did the same and then they finally pulled away from each other.

"Best not to stand out here in the open like this," Harlan grumbled.

He frowned, first because they were out in the open with a gunman loose and then because he was—hell's bells—jealous.

Yeah, he was.

He didn't want to be, but wanting the feelings to go away didn't make it happen. He forced himself to remember that blasted article she'd written. And the fact that Caitlyn had thought he was a would-be killer.

That gave him the attitude adjustment he needed.

Harlan took her by the arm and pulled her toward the car. "Slade told me there was a problem getting info on Farris," he said to Declan.

"There was. The facility wouldn't confirm or deny they had a patient by that name. The court order was taking too long, so Dallas threatened to close them down for harboring a fugitive."

"Good." Harlan wished he'd been the one to do the threatening even if a threat like that was little more than a bluff. For Pete's sake, this was an attempted-murder investigation, and in his book that should trump privacy issues of someone who shouldn't have been granted privacy in the first place.

"Farris is out, isn't he?" Caitlyn asked.

Harlan looked at his brother and wondered how she'd come to that conclusion. He didn't see anything in Declan's expression to indicate that particular piece of bad news.

But then Declan nodded. "He only spent a few days at the private facility before he was released to his personal shrink."

Caitlyn didn't make a sound, but she dropped onto the seat. "How did he get out?"

"Not sure yet. The court order should tell us that, but in the meantime, we have his name and his picture that we got from old articles on the internet."

Old articles probably connected to the time he'd attacked Caitlyn. Harlan was looking forward to putting this guy right back where he belonged. It took a special piece of slime to try to kill a woman.

"Every law enforcement agency in the state will be looking for Farris," Declan added.

Yeah, but according to Caitlyn, Farris was rich. That meant he had resources and could already be out of the country or at least hidden away. Well, if he didn't still want to kill them, that was. If he did, then Farris wouldn't go far. He'd continue to stalk Caitlyn.

"It might not be Farris," Declan reminded them. "That's why we need to take a harder look at all of this."

Harlan couldn't agree more. "I'll be by the office later, and I can expand the search."

"Not until tomorrow," his brother corrected. "Saul's orders. He put you on quarters for twenty-four hours and doesn't want to see you before then. Made it official and everything with some paperwork."

Great. Just great. Saul Warner, his boss, was forcing him to get some rest. Rest that Harlan needed badly. But he'd much rather be working the case, and the best place to do that was at the office.

Harlan hit the accelerator much harder than he'd planned and ended up peeling out of the parking lot.

"Is the anger for me, Farris or the fact you can't go to work today?" she asked.

Harlan didn't even try to lie. "All three."

She made a sound to indicate she wasn't surprised. "Don't worry." Caitlyn reached over and took the phone that was sticking out of his front pocket. "I'll make arrangements to stay elsewhere."

He snatched the phone back from her and headed for the ranch. "Elsewhere?"

"Yes. As in with a friend or something."

"Sheez. Are you trying to get yourself and your *friend*

killed? That last threat wasn't a joke, Caitlyn. This whack job isn't backing down."

The color drained from her face again, and she swallowed hard. Okay. So he hadn't meant to yell at her, but he also had to make it clear that the danger wasn't over just because they were no longer cuffed together and half-naked in a motel room.

"We have ranch hands who can set up security," he went on. "They can keep an eye out for this guy." And he could do a better job of securing his own house. He didn't have a burglar alarm, but he could lock all the windows and doors and keep watch.

"If I stay with you, I'll put you in danger, too," she said, her voice catching.

"I'm already in danger. The threats were meant to send you to me. The guy was waiting in my house with a Taser." Not exactly a pleasant thought that someone had gotten the jump on him and that it could have cost them both their lives.

"Besides," Harlan added, "I'm a marshal, and until we work out what's going on, you're not leaving my sight."

Her left eyebrow swung up. "Really?" she said with a massive amount of skepticism. "You want to *protect* me?"

There it was again. That irritating nails-on-a-chalkboard effect, since she was questioning his intentions as a lawman.

"I *will* protect you," he insisted. Wanting to do it was an entirely different matter. "And so will my brothers."

Declan included. Not a surprise, but that encounter in the parking lot still was.

"What'd you whisper to Declan?" And why he was wasting time on this, he didn't know. Oh, wait. Yeah, he did. Caitlyn was making him crazy, and not in a good way.

"Old joke." A smile bent her mouth just a little. But she didn't share either the reason for that smile or the joke itself.

Cursing again, he was about to shove his phone back into his pocket when it buzzed, and it wasn't one of his brothers' names on the screen. However, it was someone he recognized.

"Ranger Griffin Morris," Harlan snarled, and he let the call go to voice mail, where the Ranger would no doubt leave a message, adding to the others he'd already left.

"Morris," Caitlyn repeated. "The guy investigating Webb's murder. He's interviewed you?"

"Several times." And then it occurred to Harlan that the Ranger had almost certainly interviewed Caitlyn, too.

"Yes, I've talked to him," she confirmed. "He thinks one of us helped Sarah Webb kill her husband."

Harlan waited for more, but she didn't add anything. "What'd you tell him?" he came out and asked.

"The truth." She didn't hesitate either. "That I hated Webb just like the rest of you did, but I didn't help put a knife in him."

"Morris believed you and your alibi?"

Now there was some hesitation. "I think so. Again, I told him the truth—that I was with you. Why?"

"Because he sure as hell doesn't seem to believe me. I guess he figures I was big enough to help Sarah haul a dead body down a flight of stairs."

"You were. *Are*," she corrected. Caitlyn paused, then huffed. "And I guess because of my history, I'm not exactly reliable in the eyes of the law."

Probably not. Even though her juvie records were supposed to have been sealed, the Rangers had likely discovered that Caitlyn had spent some time in reform school, and she'd been in more than a fight or two both before and during her stay at Rocky Creek Children's Facility, where Webb had been murdered.

"My bad-girl past is coming back to haunt us," she mumbled. "I'm sorry about that."

Despite the mumble, he heard the sincerity, and he didn't want her apologizing for her past. Especially when part of that past was a facade.

"You weren't a bad girl," he reminded her. "You just wanted everyone to think you were." Harlan tossed her a look, daring her to argue with that fact.

After all, she'd been a virgin when they'd had sex.

"You'll always be my first," Caitlyn said under her breath.

Normally that wouldn't have caused a chill to snake down his spine, but it did now because it was the exact wording in one of the threats. He'd given it plenty of thought, but he wasn't any closer to figuring out who had written those threats. However, Caitlyn was right about one thing—whoever it was either knew them or knew someone who'd been spying on them that night at Rocky Creek.

That was just one of the puzzling things about their situation.

"Why me, Caitlyn? Why give yourself to me?" Harlan hadn't actually meant to say that aloud, but it just popped out of his mouth. It figured. He'd been saying and doing a lot of dumb things since Caitlyn had broken into his house the night before.

She lifted her shoulder as if the answer were obvious. "I really liked you and knew you wouldn't just use me." She glanced at him. "And for the record, I know it wasn't your first time, but the *you'll always be my first* was a nice touch. Made it feel special."

She made *nice touch* seemed like a ploy or lip service. It hadn't been. He'd blurted it out much as he'd just done his question. And even though it grated on him to have her believe he'd used that as some line, this time Harlan kept his mouth shut.

Sometimes the memories should just stay buried. Especially since they had so many other things to work out.

He took the turn toward Blue Creek Ranch, and he tried to remember all the things he had to do. Calls he had to make. Security arrangements. Updates on all the moving wheels of this investigation. The list was growing by leaps and bounds, but he needed to add something important.

Find Sherry Summers.

The missing former Rocky Creek resident might have answers about what was happening to them now. Of course, Sherry might not be alive. The killer might have already gotten to her.

In addition to Sherry, Harlan also needed to go through the list of suspects who could have helped Sarah Webb kill her SOB of a husband.

The Rangers had Caitlyn and him on that list.

But there had to be someone else, someone who'd actually done the crime.

"Who's your best guess for Sarah's accomplice?" he asked Caitlyn.

"Rudy Simmons," she answered right off the bat.

Yeah, the caretaker was on Harlan's suspect list, too. But so far, there'd been no evidence pointing to the man. Plus, Webb and Rudy had actually been friends. Maybe Webb's only friend.

"Kirby," Caitlyn mumbled.

He hated to hear her mention his foster father's name in the context of a murder, but Kirby could have indeed done it, especially after the beatings that Webb had given Harlan and his foster brothers. Kirby knew about the abuse, had been working hard to try to stop it, but maybe his foster father had reached a boiling point.

"Rocky Creek was supposed to be closing," Caitlyn continued, "but there were rumors that Webb had found a way to keep it open. If Kirby thought he couldn't get any of you out…"

She didn't finish. Thank God. Because that was indeed a huge motive, one that made his stomach tighten and churn.

"I'm worried about Declan's alibi," Harlan confessed.

Or rather his lack of an alibi. Declan should have been in the infirmary that night, since Webb had given him a hell of a beating earlier that day. But no one had seen Declan there, and so far his foster brother wasn't volunteering any information in that department. Of course, Harlan hadn't pushed too hard either, because if Declan did confess, then Harlan would be duty bound to do something about it.

Declan knew that, too.

"There are plenty of other suspects," Caitlyn went on.

It sounded as if she were dismissing Declan as the accomplice. Maybe because of that warm and fuzzy hug. But Harlan couldn't argue with her. Declan had been barely thirteen at the time and small to boot, and there was a long list of people who would have gladly helped Sarah squash a monster.

Including her own son, Billy Webb.

"Neither the Rangers nor any of us has had any luck finding Billy. What about you?" Harlan asked.

"None. I know he tried to commit suicide, so God

knows what Webb did to him to mess up his head. I'm sure the routine beatings didn't help. Webb gave many of us enough physical and psychological scars to ruin us for life."

And Billy and Declan weren't the only ones on the receiving end of those beatings. Webb had come after most of them—including Sarah and even Caitlyn.

She made a *hmm* sound. "He had a wicked punch," Caitlyn mumbled, rubbing her jaw. "He was the first man who ever hit me, and I swore he'd be the last."

That tightness in his gut moved to his chest, and it didn't matter that all of this had gone down sixteen-plus years ago. It still stung to know what Caitlyn had gone through.

What they all had.

He hated that this attack had brought so many of those old wounds to the surface.

"I have to get some things out of my car," Caitlyn said when they passed the vehicle she'd left parked near his house.

"I'll have one of the ranch hands do it." There were plenty of trees and shrubs just across the road from her car, and he couldn't rule out that someone could hide there and take a shot at her.

He came to a stop in front of his house and was glad to see his brother Slade on his porch. Harlan was equally pleased to see the two armed ranch hands in the pasture between his place and the main house. That meant Slade had already taken some security measures.

There'd need to be more.

Seated in one of the white rocking chairs, Slade was armed with a rifle and his Glock in his waist holster. He looked like an Old West outlaw in his battered jeans, boots and black shirt.

"Harlan," Slade greeted when they got out of the car.

Then Slade's dark blue eyes landed on Caitlyn. No huggy welcome like the one Declan had given her. Slade wasn't the huggy type, and besides, like Harlan he was still pissed off about that article—which seemed close to being petty considering all the other crud that was going on now.

"Inside," Harlan instructed. And he didn't waste any time getting Caitlyn on the porch and through the already open front door. "Has the house already been processed for prints and evidence?"

Slade nodded. "Nothing so far, but it'll take the lab a while to work on everything they collected."

No doubt. Harlan was also betting they wouldn't find anything useful. He'd caught only a split-second glimpse of the man who'd used the Taser on them, but he was pretty sure the guy had been wearing gloves.

"All the ranch hands are armed," Slade continued. "And Wyatt's on his way back from the hospital with Kirby and Stella."

"The hospital?" Caitlyn and Harlan asked in unison.

"Kirby was just there for his cancer treatment, but as soon as they're back at the house, Wyatt will lock up and set the burglar alarm."

Good. Kirby was too weak to fight off a killer, and while Kirby's fiftysomething-year-old friend Stella was a decent shot, Harlan didn't want to test her marksmanship if someone managed to get onto the ranch. He considered taking Caitlyn to the main house as well, but he figured Kirby had already had enough upsets for the day.

"Stella?" Caitlyn asked. "The one who used to work at Rocky Creek?"

The very one. Harlan settled for a nod, but he saw that little flicker go through her eyes. Caitlyn had been pretty close to Stella in those days, but the bottom line was the woman was still a suspect as accessory to Webb's murder. Not in Harlan's mind. But apparently in everyone else's.

Including Caitlyn's.

"How long has Stella been here?" Caitlyn pressed.

"Not long." And this wasn't a subject he cared to discuss. Not with other things that needed to be done. "I want the road watched," Harlan told his brother, glancing back up at Caitlyn's car.

"Got two men heading out there now," Slade answered. "More will cover the back fence."

Yeah. Because that was the most vulnerable part of the ranch. The pastures had been designed to hold and feed livestock, not to ward off gunmen, and there were plenty of places where someone could climb the fence and gain access to the ranch.

"Any sign of our missing attacker?" Harlan asked, sweeping his gaze around the house and grounds.

Slade shook his head and opened his mouth, but he stopped when they saw an SUV approaching. A vehicle that Harlan recognized, thank God. It pulled to a stop in front of Harlan's house, and he spotted his brother Wyatt at the wheel. Stella was riding shotgun and a sickly-looking Kirby was slumped in the backseat.

Slade's phone rang, and he went out to the porch to take the call while Harlan went toward the SUV. So did Caitlyn, and before she even got there, Stella stepped out. The women greeted each other with open arms and squeals of delight.

"Girl, you are a sight for sore eyes," Stella declared.

"You, too. And you haven't changed a bit."

Stella touched her fingers to her graying auburn hair. "You and Wyatt could always lay on the sweet talk, but

I'm a shallow woman and bent by flattery." She smiled at the joke, but the humor didn't quite make it to her weary eyes.

Caitlyn's attention landed on Kirby.

"Marshal Granger." Caitlyn's voice was clogged with emotion, probably because it looked as if the man was critically ill.

And hell, he might be.

One of Harlan's biggest fears was that Stella and Kirby were trying to keep the bad news about Kirby's prognosis to themselves.

"Caitlyn." Kirby managed a thin smile but didn't move from his position on the backseat. "Does this mean Harlan and you are back together?"

So no one had told him about the attack. Good. Harlan wasn't opposed to holding back some bad news, too, especially since it would only worry Kirby.

"Caitlyn's just visiting," Harlan settled for saying.

Kirby studied them both. Shook his head. "That's not a just-visiting kind of look on her face. Always thought you two were more suited for each other than you were willing to let on."

Harlan wasn't sure he liked this turn in the conversation, and he wanted to remind Kirby about the article Caitlyn had written, but behind them Slade cleared his throat and tapped his cell phone.

Oh, man. Not more bad news.

Harlan helped Stella back into the SUV. "You best get Kirby home."

Wyatt and Harlan exchanged a glance, and even though he'd call Wyatt to remind him about taking some extra security measures, his brother and he were no doubt on the same page.

"Was that call about Jay Farris?" Caitlyn asked Slade the second the SUV drove away.

Slade shook his head. "Don't know anything about Farris yet." He looked at Harlan. Then Caitlyn. "No. This bad news is about the two of you. The Rangers have sworn out a warrant for your arrests. They're on the way here now to take you both into custody."

Chapter Six

Caitlyn stared at Slade and mentally repeated the bomb-shell he'd just dropped. It didn't get any more clear the second time it went through her head.

"Arrest us?" she asked. "Why?" And that was the real question, because none of this was making sense right now. "We were the ones who were nearly killed."

Slade's eyes were already an intense steely-blue, but that darkened them even more. "This doesn't have any-thing to do with the attack. At least I don't think it does. Someone anonymously sent the Rangers so-called *proof* that you two are responsible for the disappearance of Sherry Summers and the murder of Tiffany Brock."

A lot more things went through her head—includ-ing a *good God* or two. It had to be a joke that anyone would think she or Harlan had anything to do with what had happened to the two women, but Slade wasn't the joking type.

"Proof?" Harlan questioned.

Slade immediately shook his head. "The Rangers haven't shared it with the marshals, so I don't know what they have. All Ranger Morris would say was that you'd both be taken into custody. I've put out a few feelers, and maybe someone will know what's going on."

Harlan scrubbed his hand over his face. "Then I guess I'll have to see what Morris has when he arrives."

"Probably not a good idea for you to be here much longer," Slade warned. "As far as the Rangers are concerned, you've gone rogue and are on your way to being a full-fledged outlaw."

Caitlyn saw the slight flinch Harlan made, but she figured that reaction was just the tip of the iceberg. This had to cut him to the core, because if there was one thing he wasn't, it was a rogue lawman. She doubted Harlan had ever even had a parking ticket.

"And since they plan to charge you both with murder, there won't be bail," Slade continued. "They'll throw both your butts in jail."

Mercy. That didn't help Caitlyn deal with this. She tried to understand everything Slade had just told them, but it didn't make sense.

"First of all, there's no proof that Tiffany was even murdered," she said, trying to latch on to anything that would shed light on this. "I talked to her fiancé, Devin Mathis, and he said she died in a car accident."

"A suspicious one," Slade supplied.

And Caitlyn couldn't argue with that. Devin had indeed believed the accident had been staged, even though at that time the police hadn't been able to find any evidence to prove foul play. Maybe they'd found something now, but Caitlyn couldn't see how it would be linked back to Harlan and her. She hadn't seen or heard from Tiffany in years.

Then there was Sherry's disappearance. It fell into the suspicious category, too. In fact, it was Caitlyn's former roommates' circumstances that had made her believe Harlan—or someone else—could be trying to off residents of the Rocky Creek Children's Facility.

She was, of course, leaning to her *someone else* theory now.

"I also talked with Sherry's business partner, Curtis Newell," she continued. "And he doesn't think Sherry's away on some impromptu vacation. The hard drive on her computer has been wiped clean, and there's no money or clothes missing. Only her. He's thinking foul play, too. In fact, he hired a P.I. to try to find her."

Caitlyn turned to Harlan to get his take on this, but he just shook his head. "Whatever the Rangers have must be fake. We'll have to talk with them and sort it out."

Slade stepped in front of Harlan when he started to go inside. "Didn't you hear me? If you stay, they'll arrest you, and God knows how long it'll take to clear your names. It'd be a heck of a lot easier if you could figure out what's going on, and that won't happen if you're in Ranger custody."

Harlan didn't seem overly concerned with that, but Caitlyn sure was. She'd spent some time in jail before being transferred to juvenile hall and then reform school, and she didn't want to go back. Especially because someone had manufactured evidence against them.

"Can you talk to the Rangers again and try to find out what they have before they get here?" she asked Slade.

Harlan and Slade exchanged glances, and even though Slade didn't look too hopeful, he took out his phone and made a call. Harlan looked around the grounds again as if searching for bogeymen, and he nudged her inside. She had no idea how much time they had before the Rangers arrived, but they needed to make every second count.

"I need a phone," she insisted. Caitlyn glanced around but didn't see a landline or a cell. "I can try to track down Farris. He's the one who probably sent false evidence to the Rangers."

"Farris wasn't at Rocky Creek," Harlan reminded her. "And so far, everything seems to connect back to that." He paused, shook his head again. "And yet it doesn't connect at all."

"Unless Sherry or Tiffany saw something to do with Webb's murder." Caitlyn hadn't tossed that out there off-the-cuff. She'd had days to go over every single scenario, and that was one of them. "If they did, then maybe Sarah's confession brought this all back to the surface, and now her accomplice is trying to tie up loose ends."

Harlan didn't disagree. Nor did he make any move to give her a phone. "Maybe Farris is behind Tiffany's car accident and Sherry's disappearance. He could have done that as a way to draw you out."

Maybe. She had practically been in hiding prior to that. Always moving and working mainly from home. And the threats and suspicious activity had indeed brought her out into the open. It sickened her to think that Farris could have used her old childhood connections to do that.

"I need a phone," she repeated. "I can find out when Farris left the private institution."

But even the timing might not give him an alibi for these crimes. With his money, he could have hired someone to kill Tiffany and stage it to look like a car accident.

But that didn't make sense.

"If Farris had killed Tiffany to draw me out, he would have wanted me to know it was murder. It's the same for Sherry. A disappearance doesn't have the same emotional punch as murder."

Harlan made a sound of agreement, and he looked at her. Their gazes connected, but she hadn't needed that connection to know he was exhausted and frustrated.

Just as she was. He forced out a long, weary breath and ran his fingers down the length of her arm.

It was far more comforting than it should have been.

So was the gentle grip he put on her wrist before his hand slipped into hers. Despite the mess they were in, she managed a weak smile.

And that was how Slade found them when he stepped into the entry with them. His expression stayed stony, but his eyebrows rose a fraction.

"Reliving the past?" he asked, and the tone of his voice wasn't friendly.

Caitlyn and Harlan moved away from each other. Not that they could go far. The entry was small, barely five feet across.

"I'm guessing you have something to tell us?" Harlan snapped at his brother.

"Yeah. Any chance either of you was near the site of Tiffany's car wreck?" Slade asked.

"No," Caitlyn and Harlan answered at the same time.

"Didn't figure you were, but someone sent the Rangers two eyewitness accounts that say otherwise."

"The eyewitnesses are lying." Which might be easy to prove if she and Harlan had solid alibis. Judging from Slade's expression, though, that wasn't all the news he had for them. "What else do the Rangers have?" she asked.

"My source says there are emails. Lots of them. From both of you to Sherry. And in those emails, you threaten her to stay quiet."

Despite the bone-weary fatigue, that sent a roar of anger through her. "Stay quiet about what?"

Slade shook his head. "Not sure, but I'm betting it has something to do with the Webb investigation."

Yeah, it almost certainly did. "But I didn't send any

emails. In fact, the only reason I tried to contact Sherry was because of the threats I'd received."

"And I haven't been in touch with her at all," Harlan confirmed. "In fact, I didn't even know she was missing until Caitlyn showed up at my house in the middle of the night."

"I'll get someone on the emails," Slade explained. "And disproving those two eyewitnesses. Still, I think you should both lie low—away from the Rangers— because someone's clearly trying to frame you, and it's my guess they're doing that to take you out of commission."

So they couldn't investigate whatever the heck was happening to them.

She looked at Harlan to see what his take was, but his phone buzzed before he could say anything. "It's Sergeant Tinsley from Cross Creek."

Caitlyn immediately shifted her attention to the call, and she hoped like the devil that it was good news. Maybe they'd even managed to catch the ski-masked guy who'd shot at them.

"Marshal McKinney," Harlan answered, and she could hear the hope in his voice, too. They so needed a break.

But it wasn't exactly relief or good news that she saw in Harlan's body language. Caitlyn couldn't hear what Tinsley had said to make Harlan's forehead bunch up, but she figured it meant their attacker was still at large.

"Thanks for letting me know," Harlan said to Tinsley. "And call me the minute you find him." He ended the call and looked at her. "They got a print off the threatening note that was left on the steering wheel of the truck."

That was the last thing Caitlyn had expected, especially since Tinsley had already told them the cab of the truck was clean—no sign of anything they could use to confirm the identity of their attacker.

"The print belonged to Billy Webb," Harlan added.

Caitlyn didn't even try to stop the sound of surprise she made. Billy—Sarah and Jonah Webb's son. And a prime suspect as his mother's accomplice in the murder. Better yet, he was the one suspect the Rangers hadn't been able to find or interview.

"Billy," Slade repeated. "This is the first time he's surfaced since his father's body was found."

"First time he's surfaced in years," Harlan agreed. "He hasn't been using a credit card or bank account. No current driver's license either. Even his own mother claims she hasn't heard from him. The guy's been off the grid for years—so long in fact that I thought he might be dead."

Yes, and that was why the attack and the threats didn't make sense. "Why would he come after Harlan and me—especially like this?"

All three of them stayed quiet a moment, obviously giving that some thought. "Maybe he wants revenge," Slade finally suggested.

Harlan's gaze connected with hers, and she saw his *bingo!* moment.

"Maybe Billy didn't want his father dead," Harlan continued. "Maybe he's going after people he thinks could have helped his mother. Sarah's in a guarded room at the hospital," he quickly added.

Probably because he saw the alarm in her eyes. If this theory about Billy was true, then he would want his mother dead—and Sarah was in a coma, unable to protect herself.

There was no love lost between Caitlyn and Sarah. The woman had never lifted a finger to stop her husband from beating the kids at Rocky Creek. Caitlyn included. But truth was, Caitlyn owed Sarah a huge favor. If she hadn't knifed her own husband to death, then Harlan, his brothers and all the rest might have had to spend even more time in that hellhole.

"Why would Billy go after Sherry and Tiffany?" Slade asked—the very question that was on Caitlyn's mind. "They both had decent alibis for the night of the murder."

Decent but maybe not enough. "Billy might know something we don't," Caitlyn concluded. "There were a lot of people moving around the facility that night, and the window for Webb's murder is wide enough that anyone could have done it."

A chilling thought. Because maybe that meant Billy could be picking them off one by one. Still, Caitlyn wanted to know why he'd started with Tiffany. Maybe Sherry, too. And then moved on to her.

"Do you have a current photo of Billy?" she asked. "Because I wasn't able to find one."

Both Harlan and Slade shook their heads, and she knew exactly what that meant. Yes, Sergeant Tinsley and plenty of other cops would be looking for Billy, but without a current photo, it would make that search a whole lot more difficult—especially since, as Harlan had already pointed out, Billy had been off the grid for a while now.

Caitlyn heard the sound of a car engine, and all three of them turned toward the road. She couldn't see the ranch hands Slade had said would stand guard there. But she did see the approaching bright red sports car.

Hardly the kind of vehicle a Texas Ranger would drive.

"Someone you know?" Caitlyn immediately asked Harlan and Slade.

They didn't answer but moved in front of her like a curtain of solid muscle. Slade already had his rifle ready, and Harlan drew his gun. Caitlyn didn't blame them. If she'd had her weapon, she would have pulled, too.

The car came to a noisy stop, the tires kicking up gravel and dust from the road, and the driver didn't waste a second before she heard the car door open. She couldn't actually see it, because both men were blocking her view.

"You know him?" Harlan asked his brother.

Slade shook his head.

Caitlyn came up on her tiptoes and looked at their visitor from over Harlan's shoulder.

God.

Her heart dropped to the floor.

"Caitlyn," the man said. Despite the wide smile stretching his mouth, he lifted his hands in the air as if surrendering. "Long time, no see."

"Who is he?" Harlan demanded.

Caitlyn opened her mouth, but it took several moments to get her throat unclamped so she could speak. "Jay Farris."

Chapter Seven

Harlan aimed his gun directly at the man walking toward his porch. Slade did the same, and he took up position on the other side of Caitlyn.

"Don't come a step closer," Harlan warned their visitor.

Farris came to a dead stop, but he kept smiling. Either this guy was truly nuts—a distinct possibility—or else he enjoyed unnerving everyone around him, because that smile was downright spooky. This darn sure wasn't a smiling kind of situation.

Harlan had never seen a photo of Farris and hadn't been sure what to expect, but he hadn't expected *this*. Farris wasn't the sort of man to blend into a crowd. Not with that stark bleached-blond hair and deep tan. In his cutoff khakis and white T-shirt he looked more like a rich beach bum than a would-be stalker.

Too bad Harlan couldn't say with 100 percent certainty that it'd been Farris wearing the ski mask at the motel. And now the waters were even muddier with Billy Webb's fingerprint that had been found on the latest threatening note. Still, Harlan wasn't about to dismiss blondie here as innocent just because Billy had resurfaced.

"Caitlyn," Farris repeated as if welcoming her to come closer.

Harlan didn't budge in case she intended to do just that, but Caitlyn didn't move either. One glance at her, and Harlan realized that was because she was frozen in place. She was too pale again, and she definitely wasn't smiling. He saw every bit of the fear in her eyes.

"What do you want?" she snapped at Farris. Her gaze was frozen as well on the madman who'd not only made her life a living hell, but also had tried to strangle her.

Yet here he was. Free as a bird.

Harlan would soon figure out what he could do about remedying that. The restraining order that Caitlyn had on Farris would have likely expired, but they could get a new one.

"I needed to see you," Farris said. If he was alarmed by the two guns trained on him, he didn't show it. "It's all over the news about your kidnapping. Someone took shots at you, they said, and when I saw Marshal McKinney's name, I did an internet search and found the address of the ranch. I thought you might be here."

Hell's bells. Of course it would be on the news. Harlan had forgotten about trying to suppress the story so it wouldn't clue in people like Farris that Caitlyn might be with him or any members of his family. Of course, if Farris was the person trying to kill them, he already knew about the attack anyway.

But there was something about this that just didn't fit.

If Farris had wanted Caitlyn dead, then why hadn't he killed her after he hit her with the Taser? He would have had the perfect opportunity, since she couldn't have fought back. Of course, sometimes crazy people didn't do logical things, and maybe he wanted a fight. Maybe he wanted to prolong her fear as long as possible.

"Are you okay?" Farris asked Caitlyn. "Were you hurt?"

She made a sound, a burst of laughter, but it wasn't from humor. "That's a strange question coming from you. The last time you were within reaching distance of me, you put your hands around my neck and tried to choke the life out of me."

It made Harlan's blood boil to hear that. Caitlyn wasn't a large woman by any means, and he hated that she'd come so close to dying. Back then and again today.

Finally Farris's smile dissolved. "Yes, *that*," he mumbled. He scratched his eyebrow, then his head. "I was going through some bad stuff, but I got the help I needed, and I'm all better now."

"Forgive me if neither my neck nor I believe that," Caitlyn snapped.

Harlan wanted to cheer for her. It was hard to sound that gutsy when he could feel her trembling against his back.

"I can understand why you'd be skeptical," Farris went on as if discussing a parking ticket rather than a felony. "But, honestly, I'm just here to help."

"Help?" she repeated.

"How the hell can you help?" Harlan added. "And you'd better say it fast because you're not going to be anywhere near this ranch in a couple of minutes."

Despite his warning, Farris stayed unruffled, which only added to Harlan's opinion that this guy was crazier than a june bug. "I need to reach in my pocket and take out something. Please don't shoot me when I do it."

Harlan wasn't about to agree to that until he had more info. "What's in your pocket?"

"Something you both should see. It's a photo."

That got his attention. Apparently it got Caitlyn's, too. "What kind of photo?" she demanded.

"One of the marshal and you. Someone sent it to me early this morning."

Obviously as puzzled as he was, Caitlyn glanced at Harlan and shook her head.

"Take out the picture slowly, using just two fingers, and hold it up for us to see," Harlan ordered. "Don't come any closer."

Farris followed Harlan's orders to a tee, and he thrust the photo in their direction. Even though Farris was a good five yards away, Harlan could still make out Caitlyn and him. Her gasp let him know that she'd made it out, as well.

It was a shot of Caitlyn and him half-naked on the motel bed.

"Needless to say, I was shocked to get this," Farris went on. A muscle flickered in his jaw, and for the first time since his arrival, Harlan thought he might be seeing some real emotion on the man's face.

And that emotion was jealousy.

Great. Just what they needed. A jealous nut job of a stalker with homicidal tendencies.

"Who sent that to you?" Harlan asked.

"Don't know." Farris looked at the photo, and the jaw muscle got even tighter. "Someone rang my doorbell this morning, and when I answered it, no one was there. Just an envelope on the doorstep with this photo and a note inside." Farris's gaze snapped to Caitlyn. "I didn't know you were seeing your old flame."

"I'm not," she insisted.

Farris studied the picture again, made a sound of disagreement. "You're in bed with him."

"Not voluntarily," Harlan supplied. "Someone drugged us and handcuffed us together."

That caused Farris to pull back his shoulders, and without taking his attention off the photo, he shook his head again. "I don't see any handcuffs."

"They were there." Harlan held up his left hand so that Farris would see the reddish circular bruise on his wrist. "Now, what did the note say?"

It took a moment for Farris to answer, and while he could be faking, he seemed genuinely surprised with the handcuff revelation. "The note was typed, and it said you were in room 109 at the Starlight Inn in Cross Creek."

"God," Caitlyn murmured.

Harlan hadn't thought it possible, but he felt her muscles tense even more, and she put her hand on the small of his back. Probably because her legs weren't so steady. With her still fighting off the effects of the drug and the near fatal shooting, a confrontation with her stalker was the last thing she needed, but Harlan saw this from the eyes of a lawman. That photo was evidence of a setup.

Well, it was if Farris was telling the truth.

Harlan had no plans to believe him any time soon.

"I'll bet you weren't happy when you saw that picture of Caitlyn and me," Harlan remarked, and he kept a close watch on the man's reaction.

"I wasn't." His gaze rifled to Harlan. "Wait a minute. You don't think I was so enraged when I saw this that I then tried to kill you?"

Harlan shrugged, but that was exactly the direction he was going. "You tell me. Is that what happened?"

"No." Farris cursed and denied it again. "I got help for my mental problems. I'm not a violent person anymore."

"I don't believe you," Caitlyn said, and she cleared

her throat and repeated it. "Because someone did come to that motel room and try to kill us."

"Well, that someone wasn't me," Farris practically shouted. But the fit of temper went as fast as it came, and he scrubbed his hand over his face. "Look, I came here because I wanted to make sure you were okay and because I thought you should know about this photo. Caitlyn, someone obviously wants to hurt you."

"Obviously," she said with a massive amount of sarcasm dripping from her voice. "But I didn't need you or the photo to convince me of that. The bullets convinced me just fine."

"I'm sure they did. But what's this all about?" Farris pressed. "Is this happening because of one of your articles?"

Harlan wished it were that simple. Heck, for that matter he wished he could just go ahead and arrest Farris on the spot and force him to confess to setting all this up.

But Billy's fingerprint didn't fit.

In fact, it was entirely possible that Billy had been the one to set it up and that he'd merely used Farris as a pawn. As unhinged as Farris seemed to be, he'd be easy to manipulate.

"This is Marshal Slade Becker," Harlan said, tipping his head to his brother. "And he's going to escort you into town, where you'll be tested for gunshot residue."

He waited for Farris to object, but the man only shrugged. "I didn't fire a gun."

"Then you have nothing to be concerned about, do you?" Harlan answered.

Farris glanced at his car. Then the road. And Harlan braced himself for the man to make a run for it. He didn't. Farris turned back to them and nodded.

"Hope the test won't take long," Farris said. "I have a therapy appointment in two hours."

"I'll make it fast," Slade growled. "I'll follow you to the marshals' building on Main Street in town, and don't think about ditching me because I *will* chase you down."

Coming from Slade, that was a formidable threat, and Harlan mumbled a thanks to his brother.

"My advice," Slade whispered to Harlan. "Don't wait around for Ranger Morris to arrive and arrest you. We need to be able to clear your name in case this bleached-blond piece of work doesn't pan out." He went down the porch steps to his truck.

"I'll be in touch, Caitlyn," Farris called out to her as if this had been some kind of social visit. The man was an idiot.

Or else he was very smart.

And that was what worried Harlan most.

"What happens if there's gunshot residue?" Caitlyn asked. "Will that be enough to arrest him?"

Harlan watched them drive away. "Enough to hold him for a while."

He took her by the arm and led her back inside. Partly because he didn't want Farris gawking at her in his rear-view mirror. But the main reason was there could still be another attack.

Right away he noticed the open drawers on his TV cabinet. Things had been moved around but not trashed even though there was fingerprint powder on just about every visible hard surface. His brothers had no doubt sent an entire team of CSIs out to his place once they'd realized he was missing.

Caitlyn pulled in a weary breath and sank onto his sofa. "What are we going to do about those warrants for our arrest?"

Harlan wasn't sure she was going to like this. Or even if it was the right thing to do, but he was going to listen to Slade on this. "We should leave."

She'd already started to ease the back of her head onto the sofa, but that stopped her. Harlan figured she'd at least question that decision.

Caitlyn didn't.

She got up and looked down at the scrubs she was still wearing. "At least let me get my overnight bag from my car so I can change clothes."

He nodded, locked the door. "I need to do the same." He'd stick out like a sore thumb in the green scrubs because he didn't come close to looking like a medic. "I won't be long, and if you hear a car drive up, stay away from the windows."

Harlan headed to his bedroom and grabbed a pair of jeans. His bed was unmade and things had been tossed around. A reminder that whoever had shot them with a Taser had probably ransacked the place.

But looking for what?

More proof that he and Caitlyn were sleeping together? Something to do with Webb's murder?

He pulled on his jeans and was in midzip when he heard the movement, and he automatically grabbed his gun and whirled in that direction.

However, it was only Caitlyn.

"Yeah, I'm jumpy, too," she muttered. She bracketed her hands on the jamb. "But I was thinking of something. Whoever orchestrated this attack didn't make any mistakes—"

When her explanation came to a fast halt, Harlan followed her gaze to his body. To his bare chest. Maybe even his open zipper.

"Sorry," she mumbled.

"Not to worry. I think we got an eyeful of each other when we woke up in that bed this morning." An eyeful he shouldn't be remembering with everything else on his mind, but Harlan was sure he wouldn't be able to forget it any time soon.

The past sixteen years had settled nicely on her body.

She cleared her throat, anchored her attention to the floor. "As I was saying…" But it took her several more seconds to continue. During that time, Harlan zipped up and grabbed a shirt. "Our attacker drew me out, waited until we were together and used that Taser before either of us could fight."

Harlan nodded. "He wasn't sloppy. So why leave a fingerprint on the threatening note in the truck?"

She nodded, too. "Are you thinking Farris might have planted Billy's print there?"

"Yeah." That was exactly what he was thinking. Too bad it would be a bear to prove, but it all started with finding Billy and getting his side of the story.

Harlan finished dressing and yanked open his night-stand drawer. His backup Glock was still there—yet another piece of this weird puzzle. Why hadn't their attacker taken it? He grabbed both it and his badge and some extra ammo.

But not the condoms.

Too much temptation, and he and Caitlyn already had enough of that without adding condoms to the mix.

"Where are we going?" Caitlyn stepped back when he approached the door. Purposely putting some distance between them.

And he knew why.

Despite his fatigue and stress, that old attraction was still there, rearing its head. Good thing Caitlyn knew it'd be stupid and reckless for them to act on it. But not acting on it would test them to the limits.

Because they were going to be attached at the hip, so to speak.

He opened his mouth to tell her they were heading to a place that Declan owned, but then he stopped and glanced around the room. Their attacker had clearly had some time to look for whatever he'd been looking for, but he'd also had time to plant a listening device. That was a long shot, of course, since the person probably thought he and Caitlyn wouldn't live long enough to return to his house, but it was a chance Harlan didn't want to take.

"I'll tell you when we're out of here," he whispered.

Caitlyn's eyes widened, and she, too, made a sweeping glance around the room. That also got her moving pretty darn fast, and they made it to the door before his phone buzzed.

"Please tell me there's not a problem with Farris," Caitlyn mumbled.

Harlan shook his head and stared at the caller's name on the screen. It was a name he recognized, but barely. "It's Curtis Newell."

The business partner of the missing woman, Sherry Summers.

"I didn't know you knew him," Caitlyn said, looking at the screen.

"I don't." Harlan hit the answer button. "Marshal McKinney."

"Marshal." The man sounded relieved or something. "I got your number from the Marshals Service because I'm trying to get in touch with Caitlyn Barnes. I heard about the shooting."

Harlan groaned. God knew how many people had

heard and how many welfare-check calls like this there'd be. He didn't have time for them.

"Caitlyn's okay," Harlan assured the man.

"That's good, but it's not why I'm calling." Curtis said it so quickly that his words ran together. "I really need to speak with her."

Okay. Not a welfare check. In fact, this guy sounded frantic.

Harlan glanced at her, and she motioned for him to put the call on speaker. He did.

"I'm here, Curtis," Caitlyn said. "What's wrong? Have you found Sherry?"

"No, we haven't found her. But there's plenty wrong. God, Caitlyn, what the hell's going on?"

Harlan didn't like the sound of that, and judging from the way Caitlyn pulled in her breath, neither did she. "What happened?" she asked.

"I went over to Sherry's condo to check her mail and see if there were any messages on her answering machine. I've been doing that since she went missing. Someone had trashed the place and left her a threatening note."

Great day in the morning. If these were connected, then their attacker had been very busy. "What did the threat say?"

He heard Curtis's hard, quick breaths. "'This isn't over. You're a dead woman.'"

Caitlyn pressed her fingers to her mouth, but it didn't stop the soft gasp she made. That was because it was the identical threat that had been left for her in the truck.

"But that's not all," Curtis went on. "I just got a call from Devin Mathis. You know who he is?"

Yet another name that was familiar to Harlan, but he didn't know why.

"He was engaged to Tiffany Brock, a former resident at Rocky Creek who died in a car accident."

"Devin says she was murdered," Curtis corrected. "And he got a note, too. Someone left it on his car this morning. Not a threat exactly—the note was just one word. *Dead.*"

As a lawman, Harlan forced himself to look at the logistics of this. He and Caitlyn had been in Cross Creek, but if he remembered correctly, Sherry's condo and business were in Houston. So that meant their attacker likely had an accomplice. Or else had hired someone to do his dirty work. Because that was too much ground for one person to cover in that short period of time.

"Did the cops get any prints?" Caitlyn asked Curtis. Her voice was shaking as much as her hands were.

"Two—they were both on the notes that were sent to Devin and the one left in Sherry's condo. That's why I had to talk to you. I have to know what's going on."

"I don't know what's happening," she answered. "Was it Billy Webb's prints on the threat?"

"No." His breath seemed to shudder. "Caitlyn, it was yours and Marshal McKinney's. Did you two do something to Sherry? Are you trying to silence her?"

Oh, man. That hit him hard.

"No," Harlan and Caitlyn answered in unison. She looked at him, shook her head. "How could that have happened?"

Harlan didn't have any more answers for her than he did Curtis Newell. That was bad enough, but then he heard the sound of an approaching vehicle. One glance out the window, and he saw it was Ranger Morris. Not alone either. There were two other Rangers with him— and they'd likely come to arrest Caitlyn and him.

This was all a setup, of course, and the evidence was

growing. Harlan seriously doubted that the cops who'd found the prints on those notes had withheld that evidence. If the Rangers hadn't heard it, they soon would.

"We'll have to call you back," Harlan said to Curtis.

"No—" Curtis insisted.

But Harlan ended the call anyway. "Come on." Harlan took Caitlyn by the arm and headed for the back door. "We have to leave now."

Chapter Eight

Caitlyn didn't even ask Harlan where they were going as he maneuvered the truck along the sharp curves on the rural road. But she hoped and prayed it was somewhere safe. Away from the person trying to kill them.

Away from the Rangers, too.

With everything else going on, it could be downright dangerous for them to be arrested, since it was clear now that someone was playing a cat-and-mouse game. Why, she didn't know. But here were notes left for both Devin and Curtis with Harlan's and her fingerprints and the so-called evidence someone had sent to the Rangers. No matter how many times she tossed it around in her head, she kept coming back to one place.

Rocky Creek.

And one specific event: Jonah Webb's murder.

Harlan had grabbed a laptop and some supplies from his family's main ranch house while they were making their *escape,* and she hoped she got a chance to use the computer to do some research.

"Never been a fugitive from justice before," Harlan grumbled. He finished off the last bite of the fast-food burger they'd stopped for along the way after they'd gotten out of Maverick Springs.

Caitlyn shrugged. "I have. When I was fourteen, I

got into a car with some friends. Didn't know the car was stolen until the cops spotted us, and we ran. Don't worry—you'll do better with your fugitive status once you get past the sick-to-your-stomach stage."

He looked at her from the corner of his eye. She certainly wasn't making light of it—she was scared, tired and frustrated. But in the grand scheme of things, the Rangers seemed like the least of their worries.

And complicating things even more was the old attraction between them.

But for some reason, it was both of those things that felt like dead weight on her shoulders. The Rangers—that was understandable. The attraction not so much. Well, except for Harlan's hot body and the way that hot body filled out his jeans and T-shirt. He wasn't a bad boy, but he looked the part. She knew just how gentle he could be.

Even for a girl's first time.

She'd had a few lovers since then, but Caitlyn had never had a man treat her like priceless crystal while taking her breath away with pleasure. Ironic. That her first time had been her best, and she hadn't even known what she was doing. Thank goodness Harlan had.

"What you thinking about?" Harlan asked.

Her gaze slashed to his as she wondered what had prompted that question. Oh. Her fast breathing. Flushed cheeks. And though those things were nonverbal, judging from the heated, puzzled look in Harlan's eyes, he was picking up on it.

His breath kicked up the pace, too. No flushed cheeks, but the pulse on his throat did a little gallop. His lips parted. Probably to say something to her. But it was a reminder that the man's kisses were orgasmic.

Mercy.

Enough of this.

"Um, I keep thinking that I'm responsible for nearly getting us killed." It wasn't exactly a lie. She *had* thought this over and over again in the past few hours.

He blinked. Frowned. But didn't challenge her.

She crammed most of her burger into the bag. No appetite. "If I hadn't suspected you, I wouldn't have come to your house—"

"He would have found another way to get us together."

That was probably true, but if she hadn't come to Harlan, she suspected they wouldn't be dealing with the Rangers and definitely not the heat.

Harlan checked the rearview mirror again. Something they'd both been doing during the entire drive, but there was no one behind or ahead of them. He turned onto another road, more rugged than the previous one, and drove another mile. He brought the truck to a stop in front of a log house. This wasn't a cabin. It looked more like a vacation home nestled in the woods.

"Declan owns it." Harlan got out and grabbed the bags that they'd hastily packed at the ranch.

Talk about a surprise—for several reasons. For one thing, she'd always thought of Declan as a rolling stone. Not really the home-owner type. But that was just an observation, not her real concern.

Her real concern was security.

Harlan had already switched phones to a prepaid cell and had left word with his brothers to transfer any calls to the number. He'd also made sure they weren't followed. Still, there was the obvious five-hundred-pound gorilla in the room.

"What if the Rangers look for us here?" she asked. "Declan is, after all, your foster brother."

"They won't look here. The place isn't actually in his

name. About two years ago, a distant relative of his from Ireland left it to him in his estate."

During their many chats, Declan had told her he was from Ireland. He still had a trace of the brogue, but it seemed odd that an Irish relative would buy a place like this in the middle of Nowhere, Texas, and then leave it to Declan.

"Why didn't this relative come forward when Declan was placed in Rocky Creek?" Because she knew his time there had been hell for him, and almost any family would have been better than what he'd had to face at the orphanage.

"Don't know," Harlan replied. He pressed in some numbers on the keypad by the door to unlock it. "Let's just say Declan has some secrets and leave it at that."

That only made her uneasy feeling even more uneasy. "Not secrets about Rocky Creek?" And more specifically, about Webb's murder?

But Harlan only shrugged, opened the door and punched in yet more numbers to disarm the security system before it started to beep. Obviously he wasn't planning to spill anything else about his kid brother, but that didn't mean Caitlyn couldn't do some digging. Right now, everyone was a suspect.

Well, except Harlan.

She seriously doubted he'd screw himself over like this if he was trying to hide his guilt about anything. Of course, he seemed genuinely close to his brothers, so they probably wouldn't put him through this either.

Now, she was a different story.

With the exception of Declan and maybe Stella, Harlan, his foster brothers and foster father might love to see her squirming on the end of a hook. That was why Kirby's words back at the ranch had surprised her. Something about her and Harlan being suited for each other. Well, he was wrong about that.

Despite the attraction, of course.

In that one area, she and Harlan seemed way too suited, and that didn't please either of them.

Harlan reset the alarm when he closed the door, and they put the bags on a foyer table and looked around. It looked like a place out of a glossy magazine, with its wood floors, leather furniture and massive stone fireplace. Even a work desk with a computer in the corner.

"There's a stocked freezer," Harlan said, leading her into the kitchen. "And canned goods. Just in case we're here longer than tonight. The bedrooms are upstairs."

"Two of them?" She hadn't intended to sound so concerned, but she did.

"Two," he verified, giving her a flat look. It would have worked—she might have believed the offended/uninterested act—if she hadn't seen the pulse at his throat begin to throb.

Jeez Louise.

It was bad enough that she was battling her hormones, but Harlan needed to stay sane. And unaroused.

"Why don't you go ahead and get some rest?" he mumbled.

She took a deep breath, hoping for a clear head. Didn't happen. "I'd rather get a little work done. And change my clothes," she said, looking down at the scrubs she was still wearing.

Harlan looked about to argue, but his phone buzzed. "It's Slade."

Which likely meant this might be news of the investigation. However, Harlan didn't put the call on speaker. Maybe because he wanted to buffer any more bad news they might get.

While he was occupied with that, Caitlyn went to the computer in the corner desk and turned it on. The perfect thing to get kisses and arousing thoughts out of her mind was to work. She logged on to her email account to the dozens of unanswered emails, including several from her boss, Jeb Parker, asking about the two articles she was supposed to be writing.

That caused her stomach to knot.

She hadn't forgotten about the articles, but nearly being killed had put them way on the back burner.

The first was a piece she needed to do about a captured fugitive who'd murdered his entire family and then fled. Caitlyn had managed to be in the news station's helicopter during the chase, and even though she'd already given Jeb several eyewitness articles, he wanted a follow-up. Not just a written one, but a TV appearance so they could run the footage of the helicopter chase. It would be an easy paycheck for her once she got around to it.

There was nothing easy about the second one.

Caitlyn opened the latest version of the second story that she'd put in secure cyber storage, and the headline she'd given it caused the knot in her stomach to get significantly worse.

"Trouble?" she heard someone ask.

Her own gasp echoed through the room. She'd been so caught up in what was on the screen, she hadn't heard anyone come up behind her, and she whirled around, automatically bringing up her hands to defend herself. But no defense was necessary. Because it was Harlan.

"Wired up much?" he murmured. "You really need to rest." Then he tipped his head to the screen. "Bad news?"

Caitlyn shook her head and stepped in front of it. "I'm just getting behind at work." Then she noticed his expression. "Did you get bad news?" she repeated.

Harlan lifted his shoulder. "Disappointing news," he corrected. "Slade tested Farris, but there was no gunshot residue on him."

She groaned. "So no arrest."

"No arrest," he confirmed. "But that doesn't mean he's innocent. It could mean he had on latex gloves when he fired those shots."

Caitlyn couldn't remember seeing gloves, but their attacker could have been wearing them. "What about an alibi for the shooting? Does Farris even have one?"

"Says he was alone at his parents' house, but claims one of the maids might be able to verify it."

"Or lie about it," Caitlyn muttered. If Farris had tested positive, it would have at least gotten him off the streets so Harlan and she could try to build a case against him.

"Farris turned over the photo and the note to Slade," Harlan went on. "The lab might be able to get some prints."

"Our prints," she supplied. "Like the ones on the threats that Devin and Curtis got."

Another shrug. "I figure when we were knocked out cold, it would have been easy to put our fingerprints on just about anything."

That sent a chill through her. Heaven knew what other *evidence* was going to surface. "But why is the person doing this? Why try to set us up?"

"Maybe to take the fall for Webb's murder." He paused, huffed. "But I'm pretty sure we were supposed to die in that motel room."

Caitlyn had already come to the same conclusion, but it was a whole new level of fear to hear it spoken aloud. Now the thoughts came at her nonstop. Billy had perhaps set them up and then sent Farris that photo, figuring the crazed stalker would do the killing for him.

And he'd come darn close to succeeding.

"Yeah," Caitlyn mumbled.

He was examining her face. Her eyes. And he no doubt knew what this was doing to her, because it was doing the same thing to him. Maybe worse. He had family to protect, and it didn't matter that his brothers were marshals and could take care of themselves. He never wanted to put them in danger, period.

"What about the motel?" she asked. "Were there any eyewitnesses who can help get us a better description of the shooter?"

"None. There was a traffic camera on the interstate, but it wasn't aimed in the direction of the motel."

And it was probably why their attacker had chosen to put them there.

"No sign of Billy yet," Harlan went on. "But the initial lab results are back, and it appears you and I were drugged with etorphine hydrochloride."

"The drug used on animals," she immediately supplied. "I did an article on it a while back." She snapped her fingers, trying to recall some details. "Only veterinarians have access to it, so maybe that's a way to trace our attacker."

Harlan was already shaking his head before she finished. "A large supply of it went missing a couple of months ago, and it's been showing up in black markets all over the country. Anyone with enough cash could have bought it, and I doubt we'll find a drug dealer willing to rat out a customer."

No. And besides, if it was Billy or Farris, they probably would have just hired someone to buy the drug for them so they could stay a step removed from any possible evidence.

"Do you have *any* good news?" she asked. And yes, there was frustration in her voice.

"Maybe. Slade is setting up meetings with both Curtis Newell and Devin Mathis. We'll see them in the morning."

Sherry's business partner and Tiffany's fiancé. Both had received threats and both might have information about who was behind the attacks. *Might.*

"Please tell me we're not meeting them here?" Caitlyn asked.

"No. And we obviously can't go to the marshals' building. Slade's making arrangements for someplace safe." He took her by the arm again. "Now rest."

God, she needed it. Every one of her muscles was stiff and sore. And rest would give her stupid body a chance to cool down from Harlan fantasies. She might have gotten her feet moving toward the stairs if Harlan hadn't flexed the grip on her forearm, sliding his fingers down, down, down. To her wrist. Then to her hand.

There was nothing sexual about it. Hand-holding. But he might as well have touched her in the most intimate of places, because her body turned warm and melty.

Harlan had started it with the hand-holding foreplay, but Caitlyn escalated things. Couldn't stop herself. That mouth was right there in front her. Mesmerizing. Filled with the hottest memories. So she leaned in. Pressed her lips to his.

Oh, mercy.

Big mistake. The contact hit her like a lightning bolt. All the heat, fire and intensity zapped her. Not just her either. Harlan made a sound. That male rumble in his chest and throat, and he dragged her to him. The press of their lips became a full-fledged kiss. French and everything.

Especially *everything*.

His arms were strong. She knew that. But knowing and experiencing it were two different things. Those strong arms drew her in until she was against his body. Not that she needed a punch of heat, but it made the kisses even better.

Mercy, he was good at this.

Gentle and rough at the same time. His hand went into her hair, to the back of her head so he could control the movement, angle and pressure. He already controlled everything else, so Caitlyn didn't even try to resist.

He tasted good. Like something familiar but forbidden. That was Harlan. A contradiction. Their bodies pressed closer. Until she could feel all those muscles on his chest.

His zipper, too.

No cooldown for her. Just the opposite. While her head yelled for her to back away, Caitlyn let her fingers and mouth play with fire. She slid her hand between them and touched. That incredible chest. His stomach— hard and tight.

She wanted to go lower. Actually, she wanted sex, and clearly Harlan wanted that, too, because his stomach wasn't the only part of him that was hard.

Without breaking the kiss, he moved her, turned her, until her bottom was pressed against the edge of the desk. A good angle for sex. Not so good for cashing in on some willpower. The new position put him right between her legs.

Everything aligned.

Only the blasted clothes were in the way. And as hot as the kisses had made her, clothing removal was just one touch away.

Or not.

Harlan stepped back.

Not easily. And she wasn't sure he wouldn't just dive right back at her again.

Harlan stood there. Breathing hard. Smelling like the sex she wanted to have with him. His hands tightened into fists. Finally one of them had acted like a responsible adult, but Caitlyn was having a hard time remembering why that was important.

Oh, because they had other things to do. Like clear their names and catch a killer.

So why did *this* suddenly seem more important than anything else?

"We need to agree that was a mistake," he insisted.

She glanced at the erection straining the zipper of his jeans. Then at her own nipples, puckered and very visible since she wasn't wearing a bra.

"A compromise," she murmured. "Let's just agree that it was mutual…and really, really good."

He laughed. The sound was so unexpected that it took Caitlyn a moment to shake off the tension and smile. Not because there was anything to smile about, but it was impossible to stay in sex-land with that laugh. And that smile. Mercy, the man had some big weapons in his male arsenal, and that smile was one of them. Except the smile didn't last. It dissolved in the blink of an eye, and the look on his face definitely wasn't that of a happy man.

"What the hell is that?" he snapped.

A jolt of fear went through her. God, she couldn't take any more bad news.

Afraid of what she might see, Caitlyn followed his gaze to the laptop screen. The scalding kiss had numbed her brain, because she'd forgotten *that* was on the screen. The working headline said it all.

U.S. Marshals' Cover-Up of Jonah Webb's Murder?

The question mark was there for a reason, because

she wasn't at all sure there'd been a cover-up, but Harlan likely wouldn't even notice it. That was because his attention was nailed to the first paragraph and the other question she'd posed.

With his foster sons' help, did retired marshal Kirby Granger get away with murder?

"I can explain." But she couldn't. There was no explanation she could give Harlan that would undo the fury she now saw in his eyes.

"Save it," Harlan growled. He grabbed his bag and stormed upstairs.

Chapter Nine

"Really?" Caitlyn grumbled. "You couldn't come up with a better meeting place?"

For once in the past fourteen hours or so, Harlan agreed with her, but he didn't mimic the huff she made when Slade turned onto the road at the weathered sign.

Rocky Creek Children's Facility.

Apparently they were headed back for another trip down memory lane. Harlan was more than a little fed up with those—especially the ones that involved Caitlyn. And her apparent need to screw over his family any chance she got.

"I figured this is the last place the Rangers would look for you," Slade explained. Except he always sounded as if he were picking a fight when he spoke. "Besides, it's vacant, and Joelle gave me the keys."

Joelle, their sister-in-law who'd once honchoed the investigation when it was still in the inquiry stage. That was why Joelle had the keys in the first place. Well, it sure as heck was past that inquiry stage now with the Rangers trying to arrest Caitlyn and him.

"Rudy Simmons, the caretaker, is away on a trip," Slade added. "So we'll have the place to ourselves."

"Jeez." Caitlyn forced out several breaths and pressed

her hand over her heart. "If I'd known we were coming here, I would have had a shot of tequila or something."

Again Harlan agreed. The redbrick building was practically pristine. Grounds, too. Ironic that it looked so welcoming, but if someone had asked him to paint a picture of hell, it'd be Rocky Creek.

"It doesn't exactly have good memories for any of us," Harlan mumbled. Slade added a grunt of agreement.

Caitlyn mimicked that grunt. "You never did tell me how you ended up here," she added, glancing at Harlan.

"Bad luck." That was Harlan's usual answer when it came up in conversation. Which wasn't very often. But Caitlyn already knew that bad luck had played into everyone's stay at the hellhole. "My mom cut out when I was three, and I lived with my grandmother until she passed away."

"How old were you?" She sounded truly interested or maybe she just wanted the distraction. Harlan wouldn't have minded one either, but he also didn't want conversation to distract him from keeping them safe.

"Twelve." He looked around, trying to see if there were any threats. "By then I was a big kid, and I think that intimidated any potential foster parents. Guess they figured I'd beat them to a pulp or something."

"Yeah." She hesitated, nibbled some more on her bottom lip. "I got the same attitude. The piercings and hair color didn't help."

"All those fights probably didn't either," Slade growled, and Caitlyn mumbled an agreement. His phone dinged, and he glanced at the screen before he passed it to Harlan.

"The background checks on Curtis and Devin," Harlan relayed.

That got the worried look off Caitlyn's face, and she

scooted closer to him so she could see. Not that she had to scoot far. They were all sharing the single seat in Slade's truck and were already way too close. The maneuver put them hip to hip.

Harlan ignored it.

Okay, he tried.

And he focused on the summary that his brother Clayton had done on Curtis Newell. The basics were all there. Age thirty-seven, no criminal history. He had an MBA, and from the looks of it, he'd sunk nearly every penny of his inheritance from his grandmother into the private equity business that he and Sherry had started three years earlier.

No red flags.

The business wasn't exactly thriving, but there were no signs that it was about to go bust either. The only thing that seemed marginally suspect was that even before Sherry's disappearance, Curtis had been making the bulk of the business decisions despite the fact that she was the majority owner. That could be explained simply because Sherry had delegated that responsibility to him. Of course, it could also mean that Curtis had a lot to gain if Sherry died. He would become the sole owner of their company. People had murdered for a lot less.

Harlan moved on to the next report, for Devin Mathis.

"Whoa," Caitlyn said just seconds into the record.

Definitely a whoa. "According to the San Antonio cops, Devin initially was a suspect in Tiffany's car *accident*," Harlan said so that Slade would be in on this. "Several of Tiffany's friends have come forward to say the relationship had soured and that she was about to break off the engagement."

He mulled that over, and yes, it was a possible motive for Tiffany's murder. Love gone wrong always was. But that didn't explain Sherry's disappearance and the other things happening to Caitlyn and him.

"Wait." Caitlyn pointed toward the next line of the report. "Devin *was* a suspect, but he has a decent alibi. He was out of town for two days prior to the accident, and witnesses report that Tiffany drove the vehicle during that time."

"That only means Devin didn't tamper with the brakes or anything," Harlan pointed out. "He could have hired someone to do it for him."

Her sound of agreement was laced with frustration, and Harlan knew why. They still didn't have the answers they needed to make an arrest, and essentially both men had motive. What was missing was any kind of proof.

Slade pulled his truck to a stop in front of the building, and if he was having any kind of reaction to the place, he didn't show it.

"Curtis should be here any minute." Slade checked his watch and tossed Harlan the key for the front door. "He's bringing a P.I. friend with him. More like a bodyguard if you ask me. The guy's scared."

Yeah, because of the fingerprints found on the threatening notes. Harlan's and Caitlyn's. He didn't blame the man for not trusting them.

"I'll drive back down and wait at the end of the road so I can keep watch," Slade continued. "Devin Mathis is supposed to be checking into a hotel in town soon. When he arrives, he's to give me a call, and I'll let you know. Didn't figure you'd want to talk to Curtis and Devin together."

He didn't. Harlan wanted to hear what each man had to say about the threats and this entire mess of a situation. Of course, that might be harder because of the whole distrust issue.

"Thanks, Slade. For everything," Harlan added. Yeah, he wasn't exactly comfortable being here, but he was grateful that his brother had been able to set it all up.

Slade drove away, leaving both Caitlyn and him looking up at the building. "Let's get in there," she said under her breath, "and exorcize a few demons and ghosts."

Maybe because their kissing session was still hot on his mind, that comment didn't sound as shaky as her reaction when she'd first realized this was their meeting place. The building had the demons, all right. Probably ghosts, too, and not all bad. After all, this was also where he and Caitlyn had done the deed sixteen years ago.

They'd been the least likely couple to get together—ever. Her with her reform-school background, goth-girl attitude, piercings and weekly hair-color change. He'd been the Boy Scout. Not literally. No opportunity for that, but he'd never considered himself a bad boy. Still, he and Caitlyn had found their way together.

And they'd found each other again with that mistake of a kissing session.

Opposites attract, right?

But in their case, opposites had to stop attracting. If he could just figure out how.

"I'm sorry about the article," she said out of the blue.

Harlan didn't look at her. He unlocked the door and pushed it open. "Sorry I found out or sorry you wrote it?"

"Both." She paused. "It was a knee-jerk reaction to those threats. I figured if you were sending them to me, I wanted some kind of insurance. You know, something for the world to read if I ended up dead in a suspicious car accident?"

Now he looked at her. "When are you going to send it to your boss?"

"I won't. I deleted it this morning before we left to come here."

It wasn't the answer he'd expected. "That won't hurt your *career?*" And yeah, it was a jab at her earlier excuse for writing the article that had burned him. Except to her it probably wasn't an excuse.

And he hated that he could see it from her side.

"My boss owes me a boatload of favors," she answered. "So no, pulling one article won't burn too many bridges."

Too many, but it would burn some.

"Why'd you kill the article?" he asked, not sure he wanted to hear this.

"The kiss," she readily admitted.

Harlan cursed. Yeah, that kiss was pretty darn potent, but he didn't think for one minute that it had changed her mind.

Had it?

"Look, you're not trying to kill me, and I'm not trying to screw you." She winced at her word choice. "Correction—I'm not trying to get you or your family in judicial hot water."

Good to hear. Not sure he totally believed it. "So, you think Kirby's innocent?"

"No." Not a second of hesitation either. "But if he's guilty, if he did help kill Webb, then I'd rather give him a medal than write one word that might put him behind bars."

Harlan figured that was probably the truth, or close enough to it, but he wasn't about to let go of his anger just yet. The point was—she had written the article. Maybe just days ago. And it was still too recent to have him forgive and forget.

His phone buzzed, and when he answered it, Harlan

heard Slade's voice. "Curtis Newell's driving up to the building now."

Showtime. Or rather interview time. Harlan put his phone away and popped the snap holder over his gun in his holster. "Just a precaution," he mumbled when Caitlyn made a sound of surprise.

Maybe it hadn't occurred to her that someone could have followed Curtis. Someone who could try to get past Slade. Plus, Harlan didn't know this man, and he wasn't going to blindly trust him. Curtis would be in the same mind-set.

Both he and Caitlyn drew in long breaths at the same time, and they looked out at the car that came to a stop directly in front of the steps. Earlier, Harlan had seen photos of Curtis, so he instantly recognized the stocky ginger-haired man who got out. He was wearing a dark blue suit more appropriate for a business meeting than an abandoned orphanage.

The second man was tall and bulky, and the jacket he was wearing no doubt concealed a weapon. He didn't come inside but rather stood in the doorway after his employer entered.

"Thanks for coming," Harlan greeted Curtis.

He gave an uneasy nod, barely sparing Harlan a glance before his gaze settled on Caitlyn. "I need to hear you say you didn't have anything to do with Sherry's disappearance."

"I didn't," she answered without hesitation. "And we didn't send her any threatening emails to warn her to shut up."

"The authorities think otherwise," Curtis reminded her.

"It doesn't mean it happened. Someone drugged and

kidnapped Harlan and me, and we think the person got our prints on those notes when we were out cold."

Curtis kept staring at her. There were dark circles under his eyes—which were bloodshot. He looked like a man in need of sleep. "Then who's doing this?" he pressed.

"We don't know. But the person tried to kill us."

"Did he kill Sherry, too?" His voice cracked.

Now it was Harlan's turn to say, "We don't know."

Curtis made an unmanly-sounding moan. "I'm in love with her. And no, she didn't feel the same way about me, but I couldn't turn it off. The heart wants what it wants, you know?"

Harlan glanced at Caitlyn at the same moment she glanced at him. He frowned. She lifted her shoulder. The heart wasn't in on his attraction—well, hopefully not anyway—but Harlan could substitute heart for body, and it would describe the feeling he was trying to fight.

"I'm doing everything to find Sherry," Curtis went on. "But the cops have no leads. It's like she just vanished."

Harlan wanted to give the man some hope, but he didn't intend to lie. "I think everything that's happening is linked to this place and Jonah Webb's murder. Did Sherry ever say she'd seen anything the night Webb disappeared?"

Curtis started shaking his head but stopped, paused. "She let something slip about four months ago, on the day that Webb's remains were discovered."

A day that Harlan remembered well. A crew working on the power lines had found what was left of Webb's body in a shallow grave about a mile from the Rocky Creek facility. Harlan had always figured the man was dead, but it hadn't been confirmed until that day.

"Sherry seemed worried," Curtis went on, "and when

I asked why, she said she might have been in the wrong place at the wrong time that night."

Harlan and Caitlyn exchanged another puzzled glance. "I called Sherry just days after that, and she didn't mention anything to me. Any idea what she meant?" Caitlyn asked.

"No. But I can tell you that she was scared." His gaze went to Harlan. "Of you and your family. But others, too. She said she didn't think she could trust anyone from Rocky Creek."

Judging from the slight sound Caitlyn made, that was news to her. To Harlan, too. And he was reasonably sure that Sherry hadn't said anything to the Rangers investigating the case. Certainly not to Joelle either when she'd been interviewing possible witnesses and suspects.

"Once when Sherry was on the phone, I heard her talking about Rocky Creek," Curtis continued. "She was scribbling down something, and later when I looked, I saw it was five names." He reached into his pocket, extracted a piece of paper. "I kept it."

Harlan took the paper that Curtis thrust at him, and Caitlyn moved closer. The names had indeed been scrawled along with some doodles, but they were still legible: Tiffany Brock, Caitlyn Barnes, Kirby Granger and Harlan McKinney. There was one other name on the list.

Billy Webb.

"I looked him up on the internet," Curtis said, "and I know it was his father who was murdered. I also found out he attempted suicide. I think Sherry was actually talking to him when she wrote down those names."

"What makes you say that?" Caitlyn asked.

"Just a gut feel." He shook his head. "I know you want more. I want more, too, because we need information to find Sherry. What if this crazy man is holding her captive somewhere?" Curtis grimaced. "What if he's torturing her?"

Harlan's stomach twisted, but that wasn't the worst-case scenario. No. The torturing could already be over, and Sherry could be dead.

Harlan's phone buzzed. Slade again. "Devin Mathis made it into town," his brother informed him. "Should I tell him where we are and have him drive out here?"

Curtis glanced behind him at the end of the road where the sleek car had come to a stop. "You have other people to see. I'll be going."

"You can go ahead and tell him to come out," Harlan said to his brother, and he purposely didn't mention Devin's name.

On the surface there didn't seem to be a direct connection between Devin and Curtis, and Harlan wanted to keep it that way. He didn't want the two teaming up to try to find the culprit for their loved ones' ill fates. Especially since they'd probably team up against Caitlyn and him.

Curtis looked at the note. "Could I please have that back? I want to keep it."

Harlan returned it and started to insist that the man give it to the authorities. That would be the legal thing to do, but it would be yet even more dirt against Caitlyn, Kirby and him. And besides, it might not even be important. Maybe Sherry was just jotting down names from her past.

Or setting them up.

"What?" Caitlyn whispered to him.

But Harlan didn't answer until Curtis had walked away and was out of earshot. "Curtis didn't mention one possibility—what if Sherry's alive and behind all of this?"

Caitlyn looked ready to dismiss that, but she didn't. "Maybe she helped Sarah kill Webb, and now she's trying to eliminate anyone who could prove it."

It was a stretch, and it only complicated things to add another suspect, but Harlan wanted to consider all the angles. Farris could be doing this to get his version of revenge against Caitlyn. Or Farris could be Billy's pawn.

And then there was Curtis.

He could have killed Sherry simply because she'd rejected him or because of a disagreement with their business—especially since Sherry was technically his boss since she owned the majority of their company. Of course, that didn't make all the other pieces fit, but that only meant Harlan had to look harder in case that connection was there.

His phone buzzed, and Harlan answered it, figuring it was Slade, who'd tell them that Devin would be arriving soon.

"Harlan?" With just that one word, he could hear the trouble in his brother's voice. "I'm coming your way. We need to get the heck out of here fast."

"Why? What happened?" Harlan didn't wait. He took Caitlyn by the arm and got them out the door, running toward Slade's truck barreling up the road toward them.

"Someone alerted the Rangers that you're here. Don't know who, but I just got a call from a friend who's also a dispatcher."

Even though the call wasn't on speaker, Caitlyn must have heard anyway because she cursed. Slade braked to a stop in front of them, and he and Caitlyn jumped inside. Slade didn't wait even a second before he sped away.

"Who made the call?" Caitlyn fumbled with her seat belt and finally got it on.

"Don't know, but you gotta figure it was Curtis," Slade answered. "The call was made just seconds after he walked out of the meeting."

Hell, Harlan should have seen this one coming, but he'd figured that Curtis just wanted answers, too.

But maybe not.

"Curtis might have set us up," Harlan speculated. But he had to rethink that. If Curtis had simply wanted them arrested, he could have made the call before the meeting. In fact, he could have made it the moment he knew their location.

"Maybe Curtis wanted to find out what we knew." Caitlyn tossed out the words. "So he could either find Sherry or try to cover his tracks."

It was downright spooky how often they seemed to be on the same wavelength.

"So if Curtis is behind the attacks, then how does Tiffany's accident fit into all of this?" Slade asked.

"Maybe it doesn't fit, but Curtis could have used it," Harlan said and Caitlyn murmured an agreement. "Curtis would have known about the accident, and manufactured the threats and such to make it seem as if the two are connected."

In his experience people were often willing to do any- and everything to cover their tracks when a death was involved. But Harlan didn't want to start pointing the finger at Curtis simply because he'd called the authorities on them. And besides, maybe he hadn't.

Maybe it was Devin.

Before Harlan could even voice that, Slade's phone buzzed again. "Devin Mathis," he announced, and handed the phone to Harlan. Probably because Slade was practically flying down the country road.

"Marshal McKinney," Harlan answered, and he put it on speaker so Slade and Caitlyn could hear. "We're going to have to reschedule our meeting—"

"Maybe not," Devin answered. "In fact, I don't think we can reschedule. I'm still in town at the hotel and was on my way out the door for our meeting when I got a visitor."

Probably the Texas Rangers. It wouldn't be that much of a stretch for them to put a tail on Devin on the off chance that he could lead them to Caitlyn and him.

"He says it's important," Devin went on, "that he needs to talk to you right away. And he doesn't want to go out to Rocky Creek to do it."

Surprise went through Caitlyn's eyes. "Is the guy's name Ranger Griffin Morris?"

"No," Devin immediately answered. "This guy's not a lawman. Says his name is Billy Webb."

Of all the names Harlan had expected Devin to say, that wasn't one of them. Half the state seemed to be looking for Billy, and here he'd shown up on Devin's doorstep.

"Why is he there, and what does he want?" Harlan asked.

"He won't tell me, but he says if you get here within thirty minutes, he can tell you everything he knows about what happened to his father."

Chapter Ten

Caitlyn braced herself for Harlan to nix this meeting with Devin and Billy. He was operating on adrenaline now, making nonstop calls to set everything up. He clearly had a need to get whatever information Billy might have, but she figured any second Harlan would remember that she was in the truck with them and that it might not be *safe* for her to go face-to-face with Billy. And then Harlan would backtrack.

She hoped he didn't.

Because she was as anxious as Harlan and Slade to figure out what was going on. Maybe the info that Billy wanted to share with them wouldn't come with a huge price tag.

Harlan finished his latest call to Dallas, made a sweeping glance on both sides of the road leading into Rocky Creek. No one was following them, but the town was just ahead. Rocky Creek wasn't a big town, but there'd be people and traffic, both of which would make this trip hard on the nerves. Still, it had to be done.

"Dallas is on the way," he relayed to them. "I'll call the sheriff if things don't look right at the hotel."

"If you call him, he'll have to arrest us." The reminder wasn't necessary, but she said it anyway. Caitlyn didn't want to end up behind bars—that would put an end to this meeting in the worst way possible.

Well, one of the worst.

If Billy was a killer, then an arrest might be the least of their worries.

"Why the hell would Billy go to Devin?" Slade asked. He took the turn onto Main Street and drove toward the town center.

Caitlyn had already asked herself that question. Harlan, no doubt, too. "It only makes sense if he's connected to Tiffany or her car accident."

Harlan looked at her then, and she saw the trouble brewing in his eyes. "You'll wait in the truck with Slade. I'll go in and talk to Devin and Billy." And it wasn't exactly a suggestion.

"Billy might say things to me that he won't tell you," she fired back.

"Then those are things I won't get to hear, because you're not going anywhere near him."

So, this was the nixing that she'd braced herself for. Caitlyn tried to figure out a way around it—she really wanted to confront Billy face-to-face. But Harlan wasn't going to budge, and considering that Slade's expression was even steelier than usual, he was backing up Harlan on this.

"At least use your cell to call Slade, and then keep the phone on so I can listen that way."

If Harlan heard her suggestion, he didn't acknowledge it. He had his attention nailed to the hotel. During her days at the orphanage, the building had once been a private residence, but now it had been converted into a cozy bed-and-breakfast called the Bluebonnet Inn.

Slade came to a stop, not directly in front of the place but yards away. No sign of either Devin or Billy, but there were other vehicles parked on the street and two in the small heavily treed area on the far side of the inn. There was also a trickle of traffic in front of and behind them.

Too many places for someone to hide and wait to attack.

"Get down on the seat," Harlan warned her, and he eased his hand over his Glock before he opened the door.

"Be careful," she warned him right back.

But Harlan barely made it a step when the front door to the inn flew open, and Caitlyn saw a man run onto the porch. Not Billy, but Devin. She'd never actually met the man, but she'd seen plenty of photos, and he lived up to his rich preppy image in his khakis and white shirt. However, his expression wasn't preppy or rich but rather that of a concerned man.

"Billy left out back." Devin's voice wasn't a shout exactly, but it was close, and he pointed in the direction of the two vehicles beneath the sprawling oaks in the inn's parking lot. "That's his car."

Not exactly the economy vehicle she'd expected, but rather a Mercedes. Maybe Billy had come up in the world.

With his gun drawn, Slade stepped from the truck. "I'll go after him," he said to Harlan. "You wait here with Caitlyn."

Slade jumped the picket fence and hurried across the perfectly manicured lawn toward the cars, but Devin didn't follow him. He came down the steps and made a beeline for Harlan and her.

"Why did Billy leave?" Harlan asked. His tone wasn't friendly, and he, too, had his gun drawn.

Devin shook his head. His breath was gusting, and his forehead was bunched up. "He got a call, and it must have spooked him or something. He didn't even say anything. He just started running."

Maybe a phone call from the person he was working with—or trying to set Billy up. Maybe even Farris.

Harlan volleyed his attention between Devin and Slade, all the while maneuvering himself so that he was in front of her. Protecting her. Caitlyn wasn't much of a damsel in distress, and she especially didn't like it when Harlan put himself in even more danger for her. She opened the glove compartment and found exactly what she expected to find there.

Slade's backup weapon.

She took it and got out, but she didn't move into the open. She might not be a damsel in distress, but she wasn't stupid either.

Harlan shot her a *get back in* glare, but she ignored it. "What did Billy plan to tell us?" she asked Devin.

She figured Devin would just shake his head, but he didn't. "He said he was being set up," Devin answered without taking his attention off the parking lot where Slade had now disappeared from sight. "He said someone planted his fingerprints on the threatening note left for you."

Caitlyn knew what that felt like, since someone had done the same to Harlan and her, but that didn't make Billy innocent. "How'd the person get his prints so he could do that?"

"He told me it could have even been something he actually touched. He remembers a waiter at a restaurant handing him a menu that had a piece of paper on the back of it to cover up some dishes that the waiter claimed were no longer available."

"Someone posed as a waiter to get his fingerprints?" Harlan didn't sound any more convinced than she was.

Devin nodded. "Billy said he took the menu, but after the waiter took his order, he didn't come back. He figured it was just lousy service and left, but now he's not so sure. He thinks it was a setup."

"Who did he say set him up?" Harlan asked.

Now Devin's gaze shifted to them. "You two. He thinks one of you helped his mother kill his father and now you're trying to cover your tracks."

Harlan mumbled the exact profanity that Caitlyn was thinking. "We're not the ones doing the setting up. We're on the receiving end of a scheme to make us look guilty as sin. We're not."

"Well, someone's behind this," Devin insisted. "And that someone likely murdered Tiffany."

Devin made it clear with his glare that he thought that the *someone* was Harlan and/or her. And Harlan made it clear with his glare that he was tired of being accused of something they hadn't done.

"I understand Tiffany and you didn't have an ideal engagement?" Harlan tossed out the words.

That put some starch in Devin's posture. "Are you accusing me of something?"

"Just asking a simple question. Generally I like simple answers to them."

"No, what you're looking for is a scapegoat." Devin stabbed his index finger toward Harlan's chest. "If you tie me to Tiffany's accident, then you can try and tie me to everything else that's happening. But I have no motive."

"Sure you do," Caitlyn challenged. "Tiffany was about to break off the engagement. It would have humiliated you in front of your friends and family." That was a stretch of the truth, but judging from the way Devin's eyes narrowed, it hit a nerve.

His breath was gusting even harder now, and it took Devin a moment to speak. "Let's just say for the sake of argument that I did it. How the hell could that possibly connect to Billy Webb or the disappearance of this other woman?"

Harlan shrugged. "Maybe you want to muddy the waters."

"That doesn't make sense."

"It does if you manage to get suspicion off yourself and onto someone else."

Devin opened his mouth, no doubt to return verbal fire or at least deny it, but Slade came back into view. He touched his hand to the hood of the Mercedes, said something and hurried toward them.

"No sign of Billy," Slade grumbled, and he turned to Devin. "How long ago did you say he arrived?"

"Right before I called you."

Slade shook his head. "Then something's not right, because if Billy arrived fifteen minutes ago like you said, the hood of his car should be hotter from the engine running."

That narrowed Devin's eyes again. "I'm sick and tired of being accused of lying. For all I know Billy could have been sitting out there for a while before he came inside."

Harlan took a step closer to Devin. "And why would he do that?"

"I don't know and I don't care. I came here to try to help, but all of this has just convinced me that you or one of your lawmen brothers left that threatening message." Devin turned and headed for the inn. "If you want to speak to me about anything else, you can call my lawyer." He went inside and slammed the door behind him.

"That went well," Caitlyn mumbled. She glanced at Harlan and Slade. Then at the silver Mercedes. "You think Devin set all of this up, that maybe Billy was never even here?"

"It's possible." Harlan answered so quickly that he'd probably already come to the same conclusion. "It's also possible that Devin's calling the Rangers if he hasn't already. We need to leave now."

Harlan didn't wait. He took her by the arm, pushing her back into the truck. "If Devin is still here when Dallas arrives, he'll take him in for questioning."

That was something at least, but it didn't seem nearly enough.

Harlan had already started to get in when Caitlyn caught a movement by the Mercedes. A blur of motion.

"Is it Billy?" she asked.

Harlan didn't have time to answer because the blur of motion became a lot clearer. Someone wearing a ski mask. And that someone was armed.

He took aim at them and fired.

HARLAN'S HEART SLAMMED against his chest, and he threw himself onto the seat and in front of Caitlyn. It wasn't a second too soon, because the bullet blasted into the passenger's side window where he'd just been standing.

"Get us out of here!" Harlan told Slade.

His brother started the truck and threw it into gear just as a spray of bullets crashed through the front windshield. Slade had no choice but to get down. Harlan had to as well, and then a jolt knocked him forward, slamming his shoulder and head hard into the dash.

"What the heck was that?" Caitlyn hadn't collided with just the dash, but with Harlan, too.

Harlan's head was spinning from the impact, but from what he could tell, someone had crashed into their rear bumper. "Is it a second gunman?"

Slade sat up enough to look in his side mirror. "Don't think so. Looks like the driver got shot and lost control of the vehicle."

Hell. Just what they didn't need. An innocent bystander in this dangerous mix. It was bad enough that Caitlyn was here, but God knew how many people could be hurt. One way or another, Harlan had to stop the shooter.

Whoever he was.

From the glimpse he'd gotten of the man—and it was definitely a man—it could be any of their suspects: Curtis, Farris, Billy. Even Devin. He'd definitely had time to go back inside the inn, don a ski mask and head to the parking lot to fire those shots. Yeah, it'd be risky because someone inside could have seen him, but maybe Devin was desperate enough to try to cover his tracks.

With bullets, and lots of them.

Some of those bullets tore through the car on the street behind them again, and each shot echoed through him. Mercy. He hated that Caitlyn, he and now Slade were right in the middle of danger again.

"The sheriff will be here any second." Caitlyn was shaking and had a death grip on the gun she was holding.

But Harlan knew the fear wasn't just for the shooter. It was also for the sheriff's arrival. Once he was on the scene, he'd have to arrest them.

The sound of sirens pierced through the gunfire. So did the shouts and screams of people nearby. People who'd hopefully taken cover. He didn't want anyone else hurt today, and the best way to make sure that happened for them was to get out of there. Without them, the shooter would have no targets. No reason to fire.

"Hold on," Slade warned them a split second before he hit the accelerator.

His brother stayed low in the seat, probably barely able to see over the dash. The truck lurched forward and plowed through the white picket fence that surrounded the inn, but it jarred to a stop because the tires bogged down in the soft ground and grass.

Oh, hell.

Now they were sitting ducks.

The shots didn't stop. In fact, they seemed to come at them even faster, each of them tearing through into the truck. Any one of the bullets could be lethal, and the only thing Harlan could do was keep his body over Caitlyn's to protect her as much as possible. If he lifted his head to return fire, he'd be shot and that would leave Slade to fight this battle on his own.

The sirens got closer, but Slade ignored them and kept pumping the gas to get them out of the bog. He gave the steering wheel a sharp turn to the left. The truck tore through yet more of the fence. Gate, too. But he managed to get even clearance from the vehicle that had collided with them. Slade peeled out onto the street and floored it.

The shooter gave them one last parting shot. A bullet slammed through the back window and sent a spray of safety glass onto them. Then, nothing. The rain of bullets finally stopped.

Harlan lifted his head enough to look out the side mirror. Thankfully, it was still intact, and he saw the swirling lights of a police cruiser headed right for the scene.

But he also saw something else.

A man running up the sidewalk away from the inn. Not a jog either. A full out-and-out run. Away from the truck and directly toward the police cruiser. The guy wasn't wearing a ski mask and wasn't carrying a gun, so Harlan couldn't tell if this was their shooter or not.

The shooter could have easily ditched both ski mask and weapon to make himself look innocent.

Harlan wanted to turn around and go back to haul this guy in for questioning, but the sheriff must have had the same idea. The cruiser braked to a loud stop, the tires kicking up smoke on the asphalt, and Harlan caught just a glimpse of the two officers spilling out of the car and heading for the runner.

Slade didn't stop. Didn't slow down. He sped away. Of course, that didn't mean they were out of the woods. The sheriff had probably seen them leaving the scene. And if not, Devin or some other eyewitness would give him enough details so that he'd know exactly whom to arrest.

That ate away at Harlan.

He'd hoped this meeting would give them information to help their cause, but now it was just another note in their fugitive status. Worse, he'd entangled Slade in this now.

"We'll have to ditch the truck as soon as we can," Slade reminded them.

Just hearing the words hurt, too. Worse than any gunshot wound he'd ever had. Heck, they were acting like criminals, and even though an arrest would be bad, it couldn't be as bad as this.

Harlan glanced back in the mirror. "Turn around."

Caitlyn lifted her head, stared at him. "Have you lost your mind?"

"No. I've regained it. We'll just have to conduct the rest of this investigation behind bars. I want to go back, tell the sheriff what happened and check on the bystander who might have been shot.

"Turn around," Harlan repeated when Slade kept staring at him, too.

Cursing, mumbling and sounding generally displeased with this notion, Slade hit the brakes and did a screeching U-turn in the road. "You'd better know what the hell you're doing," he added.

He did. It was the right thing. And no, it wouldn't be justice, since he and Caitlyn had been framed, but it was the only way he could live with himself.

Caitlyn huffed, sat up and pushed her hair from her face. "Always knew you were a Boy Scout." And it didn't sound like a compliment. Except after another huff, she leaned over, kissed his cheek. "I never was good at this running-from-the-law stuff either. Last time I did it, I ended up in reform school."

"Ditto," Slade growled. But unlike Caitlyn, he didn't seem nearly convinced that this was what they should be doing.

Harlan's phone buzzed, and he put the call on speaker when he saw Dallas's name on the screen. "We have a problem." Harlan greeted his brother.

"Yeah, I just heard. Someone tried to kill you. Wyatt's monitoring everything on the police radio, and I'm listening to it as it's happening," Dallas added. "I'm on my way to Rocky Creek now, not far out, so I should have some more details in the next half hour."

Good. They would need someone on their side at the police station. "We're on our way back, too."

Dallas didn't say anything for several moments. "Hold off on that and let me handle this. Caitlyn and you should go somewhere and wait."

"I don't want Slade in trouble for this," Harlan protested.

"He won't be. If someone sees the shot-up truck and reports it, I'll just tell the sheriff that I ordered Slade to get Caitlyn away from the scene. She's a civilian and doesn't need to be in the middle of a gunfight. I'll also convince the sheriff you went with them so Slade would have some backup in case Caitlyn was attacked again."

Harlan could hear the chatter from the police radio in the background. "Ranger Morris is calling in as we speak," Dallas continued, "and I want to find out what he has to say."

"But someone was shot at the scene," Harlan argued.

More radio chatter. "Yeah, and the sheriff is taking someone into custody."

The guy running from the scene, no doubt.

Caitlyn pulled in a hard breath. "Is it Devin Mathis?"

"No," Dallas answered. "According to the man's ID, it's Billy Webb."

Chapter Eleven

Caitlyn sank onto the far end of the sofa at Declan's cabin and tried to focus on the lanky dark-haired man on the laptop screen.

Billy Webb.

Maybe he had the answers that would help them clear all of this up. Of course, he might only give them more questions, and that didn't help steady her any.

The cup of tea she'd just made herself was too strong and bitter, but she drank it anyway for the caffeine hit. She needed to be alert.

The wait and watch could go on for hours.

Maybe she wouldn't fall apart during that wait, but the odds weren't good. She already felt like one big raw nerve, and the images of the shooting just wouldn't stop. Hopefully, those images would end with their wait, and she could find some way to keep herself from losing it.

Some way that didn't involve leaning on Harlan's shoulders.

He hadn't offered his shoulder, and Caitlyn hadn't pushed. It would have been nice to be able to come unglued in his strong arms—even if that would only make things worse in the long run. Harlan didn't need her boohooing all over the place, and she didn't need to think of his arms as anything other than off-limits.

Despite the mental pep talk and her attempts to stop it, Caitlyn felt tears burn her eyes, and she blinked them back, praying they didn't spill onto her cheeks. But they did, and when she went to swipe them away, Harlan looked at her.

"I'm okay," she quickly lied. He knew it was a lie, too, but he stayed put on his end of the sofa and fastened his attention back on the computer screen.

Thanks to Dallas, who was at the Rocky Creek sheriff's office, she and Harlan had not only visual but audio, as well. Ditto for his brothers back at the Maverick County marshals' office. All of them, including Slade, were tuned to it to see what Billy Webb had to say.

Or rather not say.

Because the only talking Billy had done was to ask for a lawyer.

Dallas hadn't mentioned to Sheriff Bruce Sheldon that the computer feed was also going to the cabin for Harlan and her to view. Probably for the best, since there was still a warrant out for their arrests. Though Harlan obviously didn't agree with her *for the best*.

His mood had been past the surly stage since Slade had dropped them off so he could head back to Rocky Creek and see if he could help. Like Harlan, Slade was a lawman to the core, and it was eating away at Harlan that the only thing he could do was sit, watch and stew. The only thing she could do was sit, watch and fight back tears.

"If we'd stayed, the gunman probably would have started firing more shots," she reminded him—again. "More people could have been hurt."

Or dead. They'd gotten lucky. According to Dallas, there was only one wounded bystander, and he'd already been treated and released.

Harlan made a sound, sort of a grunt of disagreement.

He glanced at his phone. No messages or calls since the last time he'd checked a few minutes earlier, and he got up and went to the front window.

"If Billy moves, let me know," he grumbled.

But Billy didn't move. He sat at the table in the interview room, not looking especially concerned about anything. In fact, nothing about him was what Caitlyn had expected. The boy she remembered had been scared of his own shadow, but this Billy was, well, poised. The expensive-looking gray suit helped. So did the fashionable haircut. Definitely not the appearance of a man with mental issues or someone who'd been in hiding and off the grid.

And that in itself posed yet more questions.

Maybe Dallas would soon have some answers for them when he got back the results of the background check. Answers to questions like where had Billy been all this time. Why was he dressed like a business executive?

And had he been the one to shoot them?

He'd already submitted to a gunshot-residue test, and it had come back negative. That wasn't the only thing working in his favor of innocence. Dallas had already relayed to them that Billy had had no weapon on him when the sheriff had taken him into custody. Plus, there'd been no evidence in his car to prove he'd been the shooter or even part of the attack.

Maybe he wasn't. It was possible someone had set him up just as they'd done to Harlan and her.

Harlan did another phone check, huffed and leaned against the window frame. He was no doubt as exhausted as she was, but he didn't have the same weary look that Caitlyn was sure she had. He just looked, well, rumpled in his jeans and shirt. Of course, Harlan had a way of taking rumpled to a whole new level.

What the devil was she going to do about him?

They couldn't get within five feet of each other without touching or kissing. Good kissing, too. The kind that reminded her that she only wanted more from him, and more was something she was reasonably sure Harlan couldn't and wouldn't give her. Beneath all the rumpled hotness was still a nice guy who probably thought it best not to start something with her that he couldn't finish.

"I don't suppose it'd do any good if you tried to rest?" she suggested. "Might be a while before Billy's lawyer shows."

"Rest?" His left eyebrow rose.

Uh-oh. Did he think she meant *that* kind of rest? Maybe. Despite her teary red eyes, she was probably giving off weird vibes that his very male body had no trouble detecting.

"Could you rest?" And it sounded like a challenge coming from him. So, not *that* after all. He was just pointing out that neither of them would get much resting done until Billy did some talking.

Yes, it was going to be a long wait.

Or maybe not.

Harlan's phone finally buzzed, and he answered it so fast that it bobbled in his hand. "Dallas," he answered, and put the call on speaker.

Caitlyn set her tea aside and turned the laptop monitor in Harlan's direction so they wouldn't miss anything if Billy's lawyer showed. However, she also didn't want to miss any of this phone conversation, so she hurried closer to Harlan.

"Got the initial background check on Billy," Dallas started. "The clothes and car aren't an act. About ten years ago his paternal grandparents let him tap into a huge trust fund they'd set up for him, and he's been paying with cash this whole time. He's also been living in a house that's still in his grandmother's maiden name."

"Why didn't Billy's mother know any of this?" Harlan immediately asked. But he didn't wait for an answer. "Maybe she did and just didn't say."

Bingo. Of course, they couldn't ask her now because Sarah Webb was in a coma and might never wake up.

"Sarah could have lied about his whereabouts because she didn't want him to have to answer questions about that night," Dallas went on, "especially if he had anything to do with his father's murder."

Caitlyn tried not to huff, but she'd wanted more. Something that pointed the finger at Billy or else excluded him as a suspect. "Is there anything in Billy's background to indicate why he'd go after Harlan, me, Tiffany or Sherry?"

"Nothing." Dallas's sigh was louder than hers had been. "The fingerprint could have been gotten without his knowledge, as you two well know. And with no GSR on his hands and no solid evidence to point to him, I doubt the sheriff can hold Billy long. Heck, even Devin is saying he doesn't think Billy's the shooter, and he probably got the best look at the guy."

Interesting. Devin didn't seem like the good-hearted type to remove suspicion from a man he hardly knew.

Unless he did know him.

"Is it possible Devin and Billy were working together?" Caitlyn asked. "Because there was something… private in the threats I received."

She looked at Harlan at the same moment he looked at her. *You'll always be my first, Caitlyn.* Yes, definitely private and intimate. Too bad just the reminder brought back other recollections. Of that night. Of the recent kisses. Memories of everything she shouldn't be remembering.

Great. Her body reacted. The heat swirled through her. Slow and easy.

"Private?" Dallas questioned.

No way would she spell it out for him, so Caitlyn settled for an explanation that wouldn't make Harlan and her squirm. "Something that could have possibly been overheard by someone at Rocky Creek and then told to the person who's trying to kill us."

Dallas made a sound of agreement. "Someone like Billy. I'll look into that, but again, I doubt it'll be enough to hold him. I'll call you as soon as I have anything."

Harlan clicked the end-call button, and even though he didn't say anything, Caitlyn felt his frustration. It helped her a little because it kept her tears at bay. Tears and crying would only add to his frustration. Hers, too.

He made another of those sounds, part huff and part groan, and his gaze met hers. Her gaze of him was a little distorted, however, because she was literally seeing him through tear-speckled lashes. She didn't dare wipe her eyes again because it would only draw attention to something she didn't want him to notice.

"You should really think about getting some rest," he said. "You heard what Dallas said. Even when Billy's lawyer shows, it'll probably be just to get him released."

"And maybe a rightful release," she muttered.

He lifted his shoulder but didn't break the stare they had locked on each other. He did move, though. He reached up and brushed the pad of his thumb over those tears. "All those bad times at Rocky Creek, I never saw you cry."

"I'd rather have eaten glass. Tears are a sign of weakness."

Another shrug. "They're normal in situations like these."

"You aren't crying," she pointed out.

The corner of his mouth lifted just a fraction. "Wouldn't go with my image."

The corner of her mouth rose, too. Not a smile exactly. The fear and emotion from the shooting were too close to the surface for that, but it felt good to share a moment like this with Harlan. A moment that didn't involve her crying on his shoulder.

But the moment changed when he didn't pull back his hand. He kept it there. His fingers rested on her cheek while his heavy-lidded gaze melted all over her. Okay, the melting was her interpretation. Harlan certainly didn't look on the verge of kissing her again.

"Why me?" he asked.

Caitlyn blinked, shook her head.

"Why did you really give yourself to me at Rocky Creek?"

Oh. *That.* She didn't miss the *really* part of his question. After all, she'd already told him she had offered up her virginity because he was a good guy. That was true, but it was more than that.

"Why not Wyatt?" Harlan pushed. "He had the hots for you."

Caitlyn couldn't pretend that she hadn't noticed Wyatt's attention. She had. "Wyatt certainly had the looks," she confessed. "But you were the total package."

Ouch. That seemed way too relationship-y, and Harlan got that deer-caught-in-the-headlights look. Time to put this right back on him.

"Why me?" she fired back.

His hand moved from her cheek to her chin. So near her mouth. And his touch felt so good that she wanted to move into it. And maybe would have, but coming on the heels of her *total package* slip, the timing sucked.

He shook his head. "Doesn't work that way for a guy. You offered, and I accepted."

Now it was her turn to give him the skeptical eye. "Plenty of girls offered, not just at Rocky Creek but at the high school, too. The gossip mill worked pretty well in those days, so if you took up anyone else's offer other than Amy Simpson and that cute cross-country runner with the big boobs, I didn't hear about it."

And Caitlyn would almost certainly have heard, because she hadn't exactly hidden her feelings for Harlan. Also, since she was somewhat of a pariah, people would have loved to have thrown in her face the fact that Harlan was into someone else.

This time, the sound he made was of agreement. "Old water," he mumbled. "Old bridge."

"Yes, except this old water still feels…a little warm," she settled for saying.

The corner of his mouth lifted even higher, and while they truly had nothing to smile about, that helped with her raw nerves, too.

She figured that would do it. No way would Harlan keep touching her and staring at her after that comment. Things were no doubt getting too *trip down memory lane* for him. But he surprised her—and judging from the profanity he mumbled, surprised himself—when he leaned in and put his mouth to hers.

That brief jolt of surprise vanished. Tears, too. In fact, it was as if his mouth took her on a supersonic ride to another place, another time.

Of course, it didn't stay just a kiss. They were stupid

and weak when it came to each other. Caitlyn wrapped her arms around him, moved in closer and bam! She got what she'd been fantasying about but knowing it shouldn't happen. She got Harlan's shoulder, arms and chest.

Oh, and pretty much everything else, too.

Now body to body, they deepened the kiss, and the ache it created felt just as necessary as air.

The feeling only got worse when Harlan ran his hand between them, touching parts of her that were begging for attention. She remembered this touch. This raging insane need that he could create inside her.

Thank goodness oxygen soon became an issue, because they had to break the kiss and gulp in deep breaths. During those brief seconds their gazes met again, and Caitlyn was sure Harlan would realize the mistake they were making.

But nope.

They went right back to each other, the kiss even more intense. The touching harder and crazier. They grappled to get closer and knocked each other off balance. Harlan's shoulder slammed into the wall, but that still didn't loosen the grip they had on each other.

Or the precise alignment.

Harlan's beefcake chest gave her breasts some mind-blowing pressure. Ditto for the rest of him. Every part of them aligned so that his sex was against her. Yes, there were clothes between them, but she could still feel every last inch of him.

There was a serious problem with their being former lovers. Her body was trying to convince the rest of her that a round of quick sex with Harlan would be good for both of them.

Very good.

But afterward…well, afterward would be awkward and would likely put some distance between them. She didn't need distance when they were essentially fighting for their lives.

Caitlyn reminded herself of all that. Three times. And even though it took every ounce of willpower, she gripped him by the shoulders and pushed herself away from him.

Oh, mercy.

She instantly felt the loss, and regret of a different kind. The realization, too, that she was just as attracted to Harlan now as she had been sixteen years ago.

Caitlyn groaned. Stepped back even farther.

"I need to apologize," he mumbled.

She shook her head. "It's not that. I'm just trying to keep myself from going back for another round. Because we both know where this will lead if we keep kissing."

He stayed quiet a moment, giving that some thought, and giving her the look. The one that had melted her too many times to count. Caitlyn felt the tug, as if they were connected by a big rubber band that might snap her back to him at any second. And it probably would have.

If Harlan's phone hadn't buzzed.

Neither of them seemed relieved by the sound, but Caitlyn thought that later—when her body had cooled down some—they might be thankful for the interruption.

Might.

Harlan took out the phone. "It's Slade." And like the other call, he put this one on speaker.

"Hope you're sitting down," Slade immediately said, "because you're not going to believe what's just happened."

Caitlyn automatically groaned. Slade's tone always

sounded the same to her—drenched in a gallon of gloom and doom—so she braced herself for more bad news.

"The Rangers killed the warrants for your arrest," Slade announced.

Harlan and she stared at each other, and even though it wasn't much to process, just one sentence, it didn't seem to make sense.

"Why?" they asked in unison.

"Still digging for the details, but whatever evidence they thought they had, it was discredited."

She shook her head. "How?"

"By someone unexpected. Farris."

That was the last name on earth she'd expected Slade to say. "How?" she repeated.

"Don't know all the facts there either, but what I do know is that Farris claims he sent those threatening emails to Sherry."

The surprise caused her stomach to flip-flop. Not that she'd thought for one second that Farris was innocent in all of this. Nope. But the surprise was that he would admit any wrongdoing.

And why would he?

"What does Farris want?" Caitlyn had meant the question more for herself than Slade.

"Who knows, but he's here at the Rocky Creek sheriff's office, and he's talking," Slade told her. "My advice? Since the law's not after you, both of you should get down here now and hear what this little viper has to say."

Chapter Twelve

Even though Caitlyn and he were walking into the Rocky Creek sheriff's office, Harlan didn't exactly feel safe.

For a darn good reason.

They'd been shot at less than two miles from here.

Plus, they were about to face down two of the men who could be responsible for the shooting. Harlan wanted Caitlyn far from here, tucked away someplace safe. But someplace safe might not exist, and right now his best bet was to keep her by his side. He hoped like the devil that his decision didn't have anything to do with their recent kissing session.

But it probably did. And that riled him to the core. Attraction and kisses shouldn't be playing into any decision about her safety.

He got Caitlyn inside the building and immediately came face-to-face with not just Sheriff Sheldon but three uniformed deputies. Normally the uniforms wouldn't have made Harlan uneasy, but it had been less than a half hour since the Rangers had dropped the charges against Caitlyn and him. It might be a while before he trusted anyone with a badge unless it was one of his brothers.

And speaking of family, both Slade and Declan came up the side hall toward the reception area. Slade greeted them with his usual no-greeting that included zero change in his expression, but Declan's forehead bunched up, showing his concern.

"You two okay?" Declan asked, but his question seemed more for Caitlyn than Harlan.

Or maybe that was just Harlan's overactive imagination. He was still nursing a twinge of jealousy over the whispered conversation that Declan and she had had back at the hospital.

"Fine," Caitlyn lied, and she repeated it, sounding less of a lie when Declan gave her arm a gentle pat.

Harlan felt a rumble of jealousy over that, too, and wondered if he should just hit himself in the head with a big rock. It might knock some sense into him.

"Billy Webb's in the first room down the hall," Sheriff Sheldon informed them. "With his lawyer. That's my way of saying he's probably not gonna be talking much, but it doesn't matter, I guess, since we got nothing to hold him. He said he'd be leaving as soon as he spoke to you."

Well, at least Billy had waited around. Harlan didn't know if that proved his innocence or if he just didn't want to look guilty. "And what about Farris?"

The sheriff tipped his head toward the hall again. "He's in the room next to Billy Webb. No lawyer yet, but he's got a couple on the way. I figure he won't be leaving any time soon. It's gonna take us a while to sort through all of this, and the Rangers want to talk to him, too."

No surprise there. "I want to question Farris. You got any problems with that?"

Sheldon shook his head. "If you get him to confess to firing those shots, I want to know about it. Rocky Creek ain't the wild, wild West, and I don't want anybody thinking they can come in here and start shooting up the place."

Harlan doubted Farris would confess to anything that

serious. In fact, this could all be part of the cat-and-
mouse game he was playing with Caitlyn. Still, sometimes people spilled things they didn't intend.

"There's a camera in the interview room," the sheriff
added. "Already turned on. I read Farris his rights, told
him everything was on the record, so whatever he says
I can and will use against him."

Harlan thanked Sheldon and considered asking Caitlyn to wait with Slade or Declan. It would save her from
facing down Farris again, but before Harlan could even
make the suggestion, she was already walking in the direction of the interview rooms.

Harlan caught up with her, and they stopped in the
doorway of the first room. The moment Billy spotted
them he got to his feet.

"Caitlyn, Harlan," Billy greeted, and he came to them
and shook their hands. His lawyer, a bald bulky man,
got up, too, and stood behind him. "Wish this was under
better circumstances," Billy added.

There was no trace of the stutter that Billy had once
had. No trace of the painfully shy kid who'd kept to himself. Heck, he was wearing a Rolex, for heaven's sake,
and from the looks of it, he'd had a recent manicure.

Yeah, he'd come up in the world, all right.

But Harlan knew that money didn't make a man innocent.

"You think Devin Mathis set up the shooting?" Billy
came right out and asked.

Harlan had to shrug. "Who set up the meeting—you
or Devin?"

"I did, but he'd been trying to find me for weeks.
Even hired a P.I. So did Sherry's business partner, Curtis
Newell." Billy looked at Caitlyn then. "And you."

She confirmed that with a nod. "A lot of people have

been looking for you, especially me. Any reason you didn't want to be found?"

"I have a new life now," he said without hesitation. "I didn't want to get caught up in the old memories and a past I'd rather just forget."

"But something changed your mind," Harlan pointed out.

"Yes." He gave a weary sigh. "I started reading about the investigation of my father's death. About Tiffany's car accident and Sherry's disappearance. I didn't think it was a coincidence that those things were happening so soon after my mother's...incident at your family's ranch."

The *incident* had nearly killed Harlan's brother Dallas and Dallas's wife, Joelle. Sarah Webb had hired armed men to make sure no one uncovered the fact that she'd murdered her husband. Sarah had been seriously injured in the attack that she'd orchestrated and had lapsed into a coma before she could name her accomplice.

Was Harlan now looking at that accomplice?

"Who helped your mother kill your father?" Harlan asked.

"I honestly don't know, but it wasn't me." Again Billy didn't hesitate. "If you remember correctly, I didn't have much of a backbone in those days."

Caitlyn stared at him. "Or maybe you did. Webb was beating your mother nearly every time his temper blew, and from what I remember, it happened often. You must have wanted to see him get his due."

Billy shrugged. "I didn't say I didn't have motive. I did. Just like the rest of you. My father had gotten approval to keep Rocky Creek open, and none of you wanted that—especially Kirby. Plus, Declan had been on the receiving end of Dad's fists that day. Joelle, too, if I remember correctly. All of that is motive for wanting him dead."

Harlan couldn't argue with any of it. Joelle had been a resident at Rocky Creek, and Webb had slapped her for some piddly infraction. Dallas and Joelle were just teenagers then, like the rest of his foster brothers, but they'd also been lovers. And Dallas was beyond protective of her, giving him a big reason to go after Webb.

But Harlan figured someone beat Dallas to it and put that knife in Webb.

The only thing Harlan was certain of was he hadn't killed the headmaster, and he was sure Caitlyn hadn't been involved either. For argument's sake, if he ruled out members of his family—and he intended to do that whether he should or not—that left Billy, Devin and Curtis.

Maybe Sherry, too, if she'd faked her disappearance.

Harlan took a business card from his wallet and wrote down the number for the prepaid cell he was still using. "Call me if you find out anything."

"I will." Billy took out a card, too. "And I ask you to do the same for me." He pulled in a long breath. "My father was a despicable man and deserved to die, but I've spent a decade and a half getting away from the muck that he caused in my life and others'. I don't want to be pulled back into it. That's why it's important that *I* find whoever's behind these attacks so my name will be cleared."

"I?" Harlan challenged. He didn't like the sound of that. "What are you planning to do?"

"Something that should have been done years ago. I intend to find the person responsible for my father's death."

Billy didn't wait for Harlan to respond to that. He

eased past them, barely sparing them a glance, and he and his lawyer walked away.

"You believe him?" Caitlyn asked before they were even out of earshot.

Harlan had to shake his head. Billy was the obvious suspect in his father's death, and that made him the obvious suspect in any cover-up.

If that was what was going on.

But Billy wasn't the one who'd confessed to any wrongdoing. That honor fell to Jay Farris.

"I'm going in there," Caitlyn said before Harlan could offer to do the interview alone. She leaned in, lowered her voice to a whisper. "I can't let him know how much he still scares me."

Oh, man. Harlan gave her arm a rub as Declan had done, but when that didn't work, he dropped a kiss on her cheek. The fear was in her eyes again, probably because she hadn't had time to recover from the last attack. Now here she was about to face down someone who'd tried to kill her.

Maybe more than once.

"Besides," she added, "if Farris tries to strangle me again, I fully expect you to beat the living daylights out of him. Yes, I know that sounds sexist, but you're bigger than I am and can do a lot more damage. Promise me, if it comes down to it, you'll do *damage.*"

He couldn't help it. He smiled. "I promise." In fact, Harlan almost welcomed it. He had a lot of dangerous energy boiling inside him, and he figured Farris better not push any of his buttons or he'd be on the receiving end of that energy.

Harlan opened the interview-room door, and unlike Billy, Farris didn't jump to his feet. He sat there, his face buried in his hands. "I'm so sorry, Caitlyn."

Harlan wasn't interested in an apology, and apparently neither was Caitlyn. She folded her arms over her chest. "Start talking, and explain the threatening notes and how you were able to discredit that so-called evidence."

Taking his time, Farris lowered his hands. "You should probably sit down."

"Start talking," she repeated. It wasn't a suggestion either.

Farris reached inside his pants pocket and pulled out a handful of paper. Not neatly folded—it looked as if he'd crammed it in there.

"My instructions," Farris explained, which didn't explain anything.

Harlan went closer and looked at the first note, which was handwritten in block letters. *Leave this for Caitlyn to find.*

"There was a note attached to it," Farris went on, "the one that warned her if she talked to the Rangers she'd be sorry." He fished out another note. "This one was attached to the one that said she'd die if she talked to them."

Harlan riffled through the others. If he followed Farris's explanation, then one of them would have been attached to the note that included the very private sentence—*you'll always be my first.*

"I didn't know where Caitlyn was, but this person knew—one of the notes had her address. Still, I didn't want to leave those threats for her to find," Farris went on. "I knew they'd upset her."

Caitlyn gave him a flat look. "And you expect me to believe that my being upset would bother you?"

Farris opened his mouth, but then his attention landed on Harlan, specifically how close he was standing to Caitlyn. Farris's gaze darted away but not before he swallowed hard. "It would have bothered me. Whether you believe it or not, I didn't want to torment you."

"But you did," she fired back.

"Only because I got that note." Farris jabbed his index finger at the papers.

Harlan didn't need to ask for clarification as to which note Farris meant, because it had already caught Harlan's attention. "'Do as I say, or you and Caitlyn will both die.'"

Farris nodded. "And with everything else going on, I didn't think it was a bluff."

"Who sent these to you?" Harlan didn't bother to sound as if he believed Farris. Because he didn't. Farris could have written all the notes himself and could have hired someone to find Caitlyn.

"I don't know who sent them, but whoever it was killed my dog, slashed my tires and vandalized my place. Then I got this note." He plucked another one from the stash. "It said if I didn't do as I was told, then the order releasing me from the institution would be revoked and I'd have to go back in. He—or she—said that's where they'd kill me."

Harlan studied his body language. It was right for someone who was genuinely upset, but Farris was likely a nutcase, which meant he could probably lie and not have any of the telltale signs.

"Ranger Morris will want to see all those notes," Harlan reminded Farris. If the man objected to that, he didn't show it either. "For now, talk to us about the evidence that you supposedly refuted."

"I disproved it," Farris corrected. Another gaze dodge. In Harlan's experience, that wasn't a good sign. "One of the notes said to hack into Sherry's computer and make it appear that Caitlyn and you had done it."

Caitlyn made a sound of surprise. "How'd you do that?"

"I'm good with computers." Farris's tone was somewhat defensive now, but he still didn't make direct eye contact. "Good at hacking," he mumbled. "My family owns a software business, and I've always helped. And as for setting you up, I just used your own personal computers."

"How?" Harlan demanded. "And if you say you broke into my house—"

"I didn't. Not yours anyway, but I did break into Caitlyn's once I had her address, and I used her computer so it could be traced back to her."

Harlan saw the goose bumps riffled over her arms. Yeah, that was a major creep factor to have her stalker, the SOB who'd tried to strangle her, break into her home.

"I didn't think it'd be easy or wise to get into your place." Farris glanced at Harlan. "So I made it look as if I'd used your computer. It was good enough to fool the Rangers anyway."

Caitlyn muttered some profanity and shifted her position so that she was even closer to him. Harlan figured it would just rile Farris even further or set him off, but after all the violations Farris had just confessed to, that seemed like a plus. So Harlan slid his arm around Caitlyn's waist and eased her to him. Until they were side by side, facing down this SOB who'd made their lives miserable.

"If I hadn't told the Rangers what I'd done, they'd still be after you." And Farris's eyes narrowed when he said that.

"If you hadn't lied in the first place, the Rangers would have had no reason to suspect us." Harlan didn't intend to give this guy any credit for clearing up some-thing he'd helped set up.

"Did this note writer ever contact you personally?" Harlan asked.

"No. Just through the notes." Farris hesitated. "But I figured it was one of you. Or maybe Devin or Curtis. I don't have a motive to kill Tiffany in a fake car accident."

"You didn't have a motive to set me up," Harlan re-minded him. "Other than the so-called threats you re-ceived. But you did it anyway."

"Wait a minute." Farris jumped to his feet. "You think I killed Tiffany? I didn't," he insisted before Harlan could answer. "I figure she was a pawn, just like I was."

Harlan gave that pawn theory some thought. Not Far-ris as a pawn but Tiffany as one. Maybe she had been if her fiancé, Devin, had murdered her and then tried to fix it so that it appeared connected to Rocky Creek.

"What about Sherry?" Caitlyn pressed. "Is she a pawn, too?"

"I don't know." With his mini fit of temper apparently exhausted, Farris sank back onto the chair. "But I found some strange things when I hacked into her computer."

"Like what?" And Harlan hoped whatever it was, Far-ris had kept copies, because Curtis had already told them that Sherry's hard drive had been wiped clean.

"She had notes, like a computer diary or something." Eyes still narrowed, he looked at Caitlyn. "Sherry wrote that she'd overheard you and Harlan that night in the basement."

Harlan felt the muscles in her body jerk. His prob-ably did, too. *"That night?"* But he already knew what Farris meant.

"She said she was looking for a place to have a smoke,

and she heard what you said to Caitlyn. Afterward. The line you said about her being your first."

Not a line, but Harlan had no intention of correcting him. At least now they knew who at Rocky Creek had overheard them. So did that mean Sherry had written those threatening notes? Harlan glanced at Caitlyn and saw the same question in her eyes.

"What else was in Sherry's files?" Caitlyn asked.

"That's just it—nothing that I would expect to find there. No files about her business or anyone else personal in her life. It was all about Tiffany's car accident and how she wondered if it was connected to Webb's murder."

Yeah, that was suspicious. Unless Sherry really was guilty and had done that to cover her tracks.

Harlan heard the rapidly approaching footsteps and automatically stepped in front of Caitlyn. He also put his hand over his weapon. But it was a false alarm of sorts.

"We're Jay Farris's attorneys," the man in the lead said. "And this interview ends now."

Farris only shrugged and tipped his head to the camera mounted in the corner. "That'll need to be turned off, too." His eyes were certainly no longer narrowed, and he seemed in complete control. In fact, he had the smug look of a man who'd accomplished his mission.

Whatever the hell that was.

Had all of this been some kind of act?

"Harlan can't protect you, you know." Farris had his attention pinned to Caitlyn now. "That's why I told you all about the notes and everything this person has made me do. I believe him when he says he'll kill you. And if you stay with Harlan, you'll both end up dead."

Harlan walked closer, stared down at Farris. "Is that a threat?"

"A warning." Farris lowered his voice to a whisper.

"Whoever's behind this is smart, and if he or she can't use me to deliver threats and hack into computers, then they'll find someone else. Probably already has."

Harlan would have liked to dispute that, but he was afraid it was the truth. And that meant he had to get to the bottom of this fast—especially if Farris couldn't be connected to any of the violent things that had happened. If the Rangers could tie him only to the notes and the computer hacking, then he'd be released on bond. *Soon*.

One of the lawyers made an impatient sound and motioned for Caitlyn and him to leave. Harlan obliged. Caitlyn was trembling, and the sooner he got her away from Farris, the better. He didn't want her to have to face the sheriff and the others while she was still composing herself, so Harlan led her into the now empty interview room where they'd talked with Billy.

"I'm a mess." Caitlyn swiped away a tear that slid down her cheek. "I'm scared. I can't think straight." Her gaze whipped to his. "And I really wanted an excuse for you to beat Farris to a pulp."

"The day's not over." He meant that to try to move things in a lighter direction, but it didn't work.

Harlan made a mental note to pick a fight with Farris first chance he got. No, it wasn't very lawman-like, but he hated seeing Caitlyn like this and wanted to do whatever it took to ease that tension from her body and face.

That caused him to freeze.

Oh, hell. He wasn't thinking straight either, and he knew exactly what was to blame. "Maybe we should just have sex and get it over with."

Okay. He clearly hadn't thought that through and should have kept that little suggestion to himself. Caitlyn stared at him. Blinked.

Then she smiled.

So maybe it had been worth sticking his foot in his mouth after all.

"We should have sex here?" Her mouth quivered again, and she slipped into his arms.

He made a show of looking at the hard tiled floor and table. It was to be part of the joke, but Harlan felt his body tense. Oh, man. Sexual jokes were never a good idea when it came to Caitlyn.

"Sorry, didn't mean to interrupt…anything," Declan said.

Harlan and she practically flew apart, and both cursed. No doubt because neither of them had heard anyone step into the doorway of the room. A big reminder that he should be thinking with his head.

"What do you want?" Harlan snapped.

"Probably not the same thing you do." Declan winked at Caitlyn. "Just have to tell you that I'm heading back to Maverick Springs." He tipped his fingers to the brim of his Stetson in a mock salute and strolled away.

That dangerous energy inside him hadn't lessened much, and for reasons he didn't want to explore, this whole winking and whispering with Declan was getting to him.

Okay, he did want to explore it.

"What's going on between Declan and you?" Yet another thing he should have thought through before opening his mouth.

"What do you mean?" And it sounded like a genuine question.

Too bad, because Harlan figured it'd make him sound like a jealous fool when he clarified it. "The whispering in the hospital parking lot."

"Oh, that." She shrugged but generally looked uncomfortable. "It's just an old bad joke."

And again she didn't offer to share it.

Probably for the best, especially since his phone buzzed. He didn't want to talk to anyone right now. Not until he saw the name on the screen.

Billy.

Harlan immediately got a bad feeling about this. "Anything wrong?" he greeted Billy. He didn't put the call on speaker, but Caitlyn moved her ear close enough to hear.

"Plenty. You need to get out to the Rocky Creek facility now." Billy's words raced together. "There's been another murder."

Chapter Thirteen

Caitlyn hadn't thought this day could possibly get any worse, but she'd obviously been wrong.

"Who's been murdered?" Harlan asked Billy.

No answer.

Harlan got the same result when he tried again. Either Billy had hung up or the call had dropped. Of course, there was a third possibility. The worst of the scenarios.

Maybe Billy wasn't in any shape to answer.

Harlan hung up and jabbed the redial button. Caitlyn moved even closer to him, until they were breath to breath, but there was nothing to hear except for the call going to voice mail.

Mercy. She hoped Billy was okay, and while she was hoping, she added the hope that the man wasn't lying. She didn't know why he would, but with all the other crazy things happening, anything was possible.

Harlan hurried back into the main area of the sheriff's office. "Billy Webb just called and said someone was murdered out at Rocky Creek."

"You can ride out with me," Slade offered, and then headed outside, toward his truck that was parked just ahead of Harlan's. This one didn't have any bullet damage, so Slade must have traded out vehicles after the attack.

Declan had already left, but the sheriff and one of the deputies grabbed their hats and hurried to a cruiser in the side parking lot.

Harlan opened the passenger door of Slade's truck, but then stopped and looked at her. "This could be dangerous."

"I know." She climbed onto the seat anyway. "But I'd rather risk going to Rocky Creek with you than stay here at the sheriff's office with Farris."

No way could he argue with that. Besides, from what she could tell, there was only one deputy left to keep watch over Farris.

Yeah, the odds were much better with Harlan.

She slid over, and Harlan got in so that Slade could start the engine and speed away. Harlan tried Billy's number again but still no answer.

The sun had already started to dip low in the sky, and the twilight and darkness wouldn't make this trip easier—especially if the lawmen had to chase down a killer.

Slade sped over the country road, the sheriff's cruiser with the lights and siren going right behind them. Caitlyn was so caught up in the tenseness of the moment that she nearly jumped out of her skin when she felt someone touch her.

But it was Harlan.

A reassuring touch, too. He slid his hand over hers. It instantly made things better. And worse. Because this attraction going on between them was getting just as complicated as the investigation.

Caitlyn groaned. "You asked what the whispering between Declan and me was about. Well, I told you it was nothing, and it was. But I don't think you believed me."

Harlan looked at her if she'd lost it. Heck, maybe she

had, but telling him that embarrassing inside joke was better than thinking about all the other things that were making her crazy. Like wondering who'd been murdered and why Billy wasn't answering his phone.

"Declan knew how I felt about you and used to tease me," she continued before Harlan said anything. "He'd come up to me at random places and times and whisper in my ear, 'Are you still crushing on Harlan?' My answer was always the same—'Am I still breathing?'"

Harlan's wide eyes took on a poleaxed expression that even the meager light couldn't cover.

Slade cleared his throat. "I can't exactly step out while you two talk," he complained. "And I really don't want to hear this."

Fair enough. It was on the personal side, even if it happened to be the silly musings of a teenage girl. It was right up there with the boy-band magazines she'd read so many times she'd memorized them.

"Why are you telling me this now?" Harlan demanded. "Do you think we're about to die or something?"

"Maybe," she admitted. That wasn't something they could totally dismiss. After all, someone had already tried to kill them twice, and as Harlan had pointed out, the day wasn't quite over yet. "But I also didn't want you to think I was keeping secrets."

"Like the article you were writing on Kirby," Slade challenged.

"Caitlyn axed that article," Harlan tossed out just as fast.

It had cost him to defend her and Caitlyn appreciated it. However, she knew it was motivated by the attraction. But even a strong attraction wasn't going to smooth over the differences between Harlan and her.

Would that stop them from landing in bed?

No.

But it would basically ensure that she'd get a broken heart out of this. In the grand scheme of things that was better than dying, but it was a sad day in a woman's life when it came down to those two options.

Slade turned onto the road toward Rocky Creek. Not cloaked in darkness, thank goodness. There were plenty of security lights blazing, and when the building came into view, Caitlyn immediately spotted not one car but two. One of them belonged to Billy, and she recognized another as Curtis's.

"What the hell is going on?" Harlan mumbled, and he tried Billy's phone again. Still no answer.

Before Slade and the cruiser even pulled to a stop, Curtis got out. Not alone either. He had his bodyguard with him—the same man who'd been with him when he'd visited Harlan and her.

But Billy wasn't in his vehicle.

It was empty, and the driver's door was wide-open. Worse, the repeated beeping sound let her know that the key was still in the ignition. Headlights on, too. Whatever had gone on here, it appeared that Billy had made a hasty exit.

And not a voluntary one.

"What happened?" Harlan asked Curtis the moment he got out. He drew his gun just as the sheriff and deputy did when they hurried from the cruiser. "Where's Billy Webb? And who was murdered?"

"Murdered?" Curtis repeated. The shock in his voice made it seem as if he was hearing this for the first time. And maybe he was.

"Billy didn't say anything about anyone being murdered." Curtis was trying to catch his breath, and he motioned for his bodyguard to move closer to him. "Billy called me about a half hour ago and asked me to meet him here."

Caitlyn got out of the truck as well, but when she tried to go closer to the men, Harlan blocked her path. He scanned the area and positioned himself in front of her like a sentry.

"And you came because Billy asked?" Caitlyn didn't know if he was lying or just plain stupid. "There's a killer on the loose." Heck, maybe Curtis himself, and if so that would explain why he hadn't been afraid that he might die out here.

Of course, the same could be said for Billy.

"Where's Billy?" Harlan demanded.

"Don't know. We just got here a few minutes ago, and we found his car like this. He's not answering his phone either."

"How in the name of heaven did Billy convince you to come out here?" she asked.

Curtis cursed, but not at them. He cursed himself. "Billy said he was meeting someone who had answers about Sherry's disappearance. I need answers, and he sounded as if he had them. Besides, Sherry always said she liked Billy, that he was a good kid. I thought I could trust him."

"My advice? Don't trust anyone," Harlan warned. He looked back at her. "Stay put, and if anything goes wrong, get inside the truck."

She nodded, only because she didn't want an argument to distract him from finding the person Billy claimed had been murdered. Still, she didn't want Harlan headed into those woods.

But that was exactly the direction he went.

Slade stayed with her, taking over protection detail,

but Harlan looked at the ground around Billy's car and started walking toward a thick cluster of trees on the east side of the property. Thankfully, he didn't go alone. Both Sheriff Sheldon and the deputy followed.

"I want a gun," she whispered to Slade. She figured he had some kind of backup on him. He stared at her, debating what to do, and finally reached into the back waist of his jeans and pulled out a small pistol.

"I was wrong to trust Billy, wasn't I?" But Curtis didn't wait for an answer. "Is he a killer? Is he the one behind all these bad things that have been happening?"

"I don't know." But considering that Billy wasn't answering his phone and was nowhere in sight, it was just as likely that Billy had been the victim of foul play.

Curtis hitched his thumb to the building. "Can we at least go inside and wait? I feel like a sitting duck out here."

"The door's got a lock on it," his bodyguard observed.

Harlan had a key, or at least he'd had one for their earlier visit. But then Caitlyn remembered that he hadn't locked it when they'd run out of there after someone—maybe Curtis—had called the Rangers on them.

"So who locked it?" She glanced back at Slade.

But Slade just lifted his shoulder. "Not me. Maybe the groundskeeper, Rudy Simmons, is back from his trip."

Caitlyn remembered the man, but he hadn't been there during their earlier visit. However, he could be the one Billy had called about. Maybe Billy had found the man's body, but that didn't answer the question of where Billy had gone.

And had he been forced to make a hasty exit from his vehicle?

Her heart began to bang against her chest when Harlan and the other lawmen disappeared into the woods.

After the past two days of nothing but danger and chaos, she should have been numb to it by now, but Harlan and numb didn't go together.

There was no sound, no warning, but the security lights suddenly went out. Before Caitlyn could even react, Slade latched on to her, swinging her between him and the truck seat, and raised his gun.

"Harlan?" she shouted.

No answer. She braced herself for the sound of shots. For anything. But nothing happened.

Her heart was past the pounding stage now, and everything inside her screamed for her to run and help Harlan, but Slade kept her pinned in place.

Her eyes adjusted to the pitchy darkness, and thanks to the lights from Billy's car, she had no trouble seeing Curtis and his bodyguard. Both had weapons drawn, too. But the one person she couldn't see was Harlan.

"He could be ambushed." Her voice didn't have much sound, but Slade must have heard it.

"Harlan?" Slade called.

The moments crawled by, and Caitlyn hadn't thought that silence could terrify her any more than she already was, but it did. She couldn't just stand there if Harlan was in some kind of danger.

"I have to go," she told Slade, and she made sure it didn't sound like a suggestion.

That earned her another glare from him. Some profanity, too. But he started moving along with her. "Stay behind me and try not to get killed."

Not exactly a friendly invitation, but she'd take what she could get. Caitlyn stayed right with Slade as he made his way to the woods. Not a speedy trip, though, because he kept looking back at Curtis and his bodyguard. Caitlyn did, too, but neither man made an attempt to follow them. In fact, they got back inside their car.

Each step seemed to take a lifetime, but Slade didn't run. He inched along, his gaze snapping all around them. Caitlyn kept watch, too, but by the time she made it to the trees, the worst-case scenarios were starting to smother her.

Until she heard Harlan.

He whispered something she didn't understand, and before she actually saw him, his hand snaked out from the tree and he jerked her toward him. It was too dark for her to see his expression, but he put his mouth to her ear.

"Shhh." And Harlan tipped his head toward their right.

Caitlyn followed his gaze and saw a faint light in the distance. Maybe a flashlight, but if so, it was on the ground, and if someone was holding it, the person didn't seem to be moving.

Was it Billy?

And if he wasn't moving, did that mean he'd been hurt or even killed?

Harlan motioned for Slade to move behind her. He did, and along with the sheriff and deputy, they began to make their way toward the light. Above them a breeze was rattling the leaves just enough that it made it harder for Caitlyn to hear. Maybe those leaves and the breeze wouldn't mask the footsteps of anyone trying to sneak up on them.

They were still a good ten yards away from the light when Harlan's phone buzzed. Mumbling some profanity about the bad timing, he took out his cell, the screen like a beacon in the darkness.

"It's Billy," Harlan relayed to them in a whisper. He

didn't put the call on speaker but Caitlyn stayed close
enough to hear.

"Someone tried to kill me," Billy blurted out.

Mercy. That was not what she wanted to hear. It meant
the killer was still out here in these woods.

"Where are you?" Harlan asked. He got them moving again.

"By the creek. Right after I talked to you, someone
fired a shot at me. That's when I ran."

Caitlyn couldn't be sure, but she thought she actually
heard the rushing creek water in the background. She
certainly heard the fear in Billy's voice.

"I dropped my flashlight in the woods." Billy moaned.
"By the body."

"Whose body?" Harlan demanded.

Billy made another sound as if he'd sucked in his
breath. "I hear footsteps."

And with that, the call ended.

"Head to the creek," Harlan told Slade. "Take the
deputy with you."

Slade didn't question his brother's order and neither
did the deputy. As she watched them hurry away, however, Caitlyn had a sickening thought.

What if Billy had set all of this up?

What if he'd done this to separate them so he could
pick them off one by one?

Maybe there'd been no murder—only the ones that
Billy was planning now. Their murders. But Caitlyn
wouldn't just let Billy or anyone else kill them without
a fight. Thank God she'd gotten the gun from Slade.

Harlan pushed aside a low-hanging tree branch, and
from over his shoulder Caitlyn spotted the flashlight on
the ground amid some weeds. The lines of light sprayed

out like fingers and moved with each new brush from the breeze.

Then Caitlyn saw the body.

There went her theory about no murder. The person was in a heap facedown.

The three of them moved forward in unison. Not much they could tell, though, because the person was wearing a raincoat and slicker-style hat.

"Keep watch," Harlan reminded them, and he stooped to touch his fingers to the person's neck.

Almost immediately he drew back his hand. "Dead."

Caitlyn's breath swooshed out. She'd hoped this was a false alarm, but no such luck. And she seriously doubted that it was the killer dead on the ground.

No.

This was another victim.

Harlan didn't touch the rest of the body or the flashlight, but he pushed the button on his phone to illuminate the screen so he could lower it to the face.

Even with the angle and the hat, Caitlyn could see the person's features, and she staggered back.

God.

Sherry Summers was no longer missing. She was dead.

Chapter Fourteen

Harlan was glad it was close to midnight, because that meant this hellish day would soon be over.

Finally.

There was no way of knowing if tomorrow would be equally hellish, but anything short of death and serious injury would be an improvement.

"Anything new?" Caitlyn asked. She stood in the doorway of his home office sipping a longneck beer that she'd snagged from his fridge.

Nothing new that he wanted to relay to her, so he settled for a grunt that could have meant anything.

She'd showered. He caught a whiff of his soap. Shampoo, too. But they seemed to smell a lot better on her than they'd ever smelled on him.

"It's my last change of clothes," she mumbled, glancing down at her jeans and white camisole.

It took Harlan a moment to realize why she'd volunteered that. Because he was looking her over from head to toe. Actually, he was past the looking stage and had progressed to gawking, so he forced himself to glance away. Not that it would help. Her image was branded in his head. Her taste, too.

Heck, plain and simple, he was just branded all over when it came to Caitlyn.

That wasn't a news flash to either of them. She had yet to step into his office since they'd arrived back at his house. In fact, she'd pretty much avoided getting anywhere near him.

Maybe because she felt as he did. If they touched, the hellish day might come crashing down on them.

Harlan wasn't sure what the result of the crashing might be—maybe sex or a good falling apart—but the latter seemed a lot to risk with the exhaustion already closing in.

Even though every bone and muscle in his body was yelling for him to get some sleep, he continued to scroll through the reports and emails he was getting about the investigation. Everyone seemed to be in on it. The marshals. Rangers. The locals from Rocky Creek. The governor was even asking questions, because Sherry's body had been found on state-owned property. So Harlan read them all, not liking much of what he was reading.

Farris was already out of jail on bond. Lots of money and good lawyers could manage that even for a man who should be locked away for life.

Billy was in hospital being treated for a gunshot wound to the arm. It wasn't serious, but the man had been so shaken up that he'd required some sedation. However, he'd be released soon.

Devin was nowhere to be found, and Curtis had had a major meltdown when he'd seen Sherry's body. According to his lawyer, Curtis was so distraught, he wouldn't be able to answer questions for a while.

Caitlyn cleared her throat, grabbing his attention again. "How'd Sherry die?"

Oh, it was going to hurt to say this and hurt even more for her to hear it. "She'd been strangled."

Caitlyn clamped her teeth over her bottom lip, but

not before she made a helpless little sound. Harlan could almost see the memories of Farris's attack zooming through her head.

"Farris could have done it," she choked out.

Yeah, Farris could have indeed killed Sherry, and his motive might be all mixed together with his obsession with Caitlyn. "We won't know for a while, but the ME thinks Sherry could have been dead for days."

Hell, maybe even weeks, because when Harlan had touched her, she'd felt ice-cold, as if her body had been frozen and then partially thawed. That meant any of their suspects could have killed her at any time, and their alibis were out the window.

"Did Billy happen to say how he knew the body was there?" Still holding the nearly full bottle of beer in her hand, Caitlyn reached down, pulled off her shoes and rubbed her feet. It seemed, well, normal except her hands were trembling.

"He said, but it didn't make a lot of sense." Harlan was hoping he could blame that on the sedative Billy had been given. "He claims he was out at Rocky Creek just to look around and maybe talk to the groundskeeper, and then he heard something in the woods and went to have a look. That's when he found the body."

"*Claims?* You don't believe him."

Harlan had to shrug. "As far as I'm concerned, he's still a suspect."

"Along with Devin, Curtis and Farris." The next sound she made was one of pure frustration.

She bobbled, nearly lost her footing and Harlan stood to catch her. However, Caitlyn waved him off and slid down to a sitting position on the floor. "I'd love to lean on you tonight, but we both know it'd lead straight to the bed."

Since it had already crossed his mind—many times—
he hadn't expected her *stating the obvious* comment to
hit him like a sucker punch. But he actually lost his
breath for a moment. Not a very manly reaction, which
was weird, because everything else about his reaction
was manly times a thousand. His body sure wasn't going
to let him forget that if he pushed this, just a little, he
could have Caitlyn in his bed.

Or on his office floor.

The corner of her mouth lifted. "Face it, we're too
tired for sex anyway."

"No such thing."

She laughed. It was smoky and thick and laced with
the fatigue that had obviously made them both punchy.
"What we need is to catch the killer, get some rest and
then…go out to dinner or something."

"I'd prefer the sex. But dinner's a good start."

He stood there, watching her and wondering how long
it was going to take him to get on the floor with her. But
a thought stopped him, and he mentally repeated what
she'd just said.

Catch the killer.

The only way that was going to happen was to flush
him out.

Caitlyn tilted her head, studied him. "That doesn't
seem like a foreplay kind of look in your eyes."

"It's not." And while it hurt to say that, he saw a glim-
mer of hope. A way of maybe ending the danger so that
he and Caitlyn could, well, *have dinner*.

"What are you doing?" she asked when he took out
his phone.

"Putting out some bait."

He called the marshals' office, and Slade answered.

Obviously, Caitlyn and he weren't the only ones not getting any sleep tonight.

"Nothing to update," Slade immediately volunteered. "How about you?"

"No, and that's why I want to shake things up. I need something leaked, but I want it to come from the marshals so it looks official."

"I can send it from my work computer. What you want leaked?"

"A lie," Harlan readily admitted. "You okay with that?"

Slade just grunted. "What's the lie?"

"That the ME found something on Sherry's body. A partial fingerprint on the back of her neck that's consistent with the ligature marks from the strangulation that caused her death. And I want you to say that the Rangers are sending someone to the morgue first thing in the morning so the print can be retrieved and processed."

Slade stayed quiet a moment. "Most people know that it's hard as hell to retrieve a fingerprint from a body."

"Hard but not impossible. All I need is for Sherry's killer to have enough concern that he'll try to do something to cover up that print."

And not something that involved Caitlyn and him either. Nor anyone in his family.

"Guess this means you'll want someone watching the morgue?" Slade clarified.

"Oh, yeah. And I don't want the ME or anyone else in the building."

"No one's over there anyway this time of night. Not even a security guard, but they do have an alarm."

"Keep it on and have someone in place to watch all entrances and exits before you send out the leak. You got the manpower for that?"

"I can find it." Slade didn't hesitate. "I'll call you when I have something."

Caitlyn got to her feet and scrubbed her hand down the side of her jeans. "If it's Farris, he'll hire someone to destroy the evidence."

Harlan agreed. Billy likely would, too. And that left Devin and Curtis. He didn't know them well, but if they were behind these deaths, he doubted either would want evidence to convict them.

Of course, even if they managed to make an arrest, it still meant unraveling all the threatening notes, Farris's computer-hacking adventures, Tiffany's car accident, their own kidnapping and the shootings.

"What now?" Caitlyn asked.

"Now we wait." Harlan checked the time. "You should get some rest," he reminded her again. Reminded himself, too.

But he didn't move. Couldn't. And he swore that someone had cemented his feet to the floor.

"Do we really want to do this?" she asked, her voice all warm and breathy.

Since he was a guy, his body wasn't going to let him think long and hard about a question like that. So he just jumped right into the mistake they'd be making no matter how much thought he gave it.

Harlan reached out, hooked his arm around her waist and pulled her to him. The problem was she didn't even put up a token resistance or offer any other questions that might force him to think. Then he kissed her and forgot all about questions and common sense. Forgot all about the other things he should be doing.

Hell, he forgot how to breathe.

Everything hit him at once. The feel of her in his arms. The way she fit against his body. Her taste. Yeah, especially that. Some women just tasted good, and Caitlyn tasted better than good.

She made a little purring sound deep in her throat that stalled his breath, and she coiled her arms around him. Soon they were plastered against each other. Until his body started to remind him just how much better this kiss would be if he stripped off Caitlyn's clothes and kissed every inch of her body.

Caitlyn clearly had the same idea, because she went after his shirt. And she wasn't very good at it. She tugged, pulled, catching his chest hair. It didn't cool him down one bit, and he finally let go of her for just a second so he could shuck the shirt off over his head.

Her eyes lit up, she smiled and she looked at his chest as if she planned to have him for dinner. Harlan figured he was looking at her the same darn way.

While she kissed his chest, touched him and generally made him hot and crazy, Harlan rid her of her own top. Her bra was lace and white. Barely there. But it was too much between them, so he quickly rid her of it and did some payback. He dropped lower and kissed her breasts.

A lot.

"Yes," she mumbled. "And so help me, you'd better not call this off when your conscience kicks in."

He lifted his head so he could give her a flat look, took her hand and pressed it to the front of his jeans. "Does it feel like I'll call it off?"

Her next smile had a touch of the devil in it. "No." She shoved down his zipper and put her hand inside. Not just inside his jeans either. She might have fumbled with the shirt, but she found her way into his boxers without a problem and latched on to his erection.

Harlan was sure his eyes crossed.

"Hell," he muttered. And while he could still walk, he scooped her up and headed for his bedroom.

"Not up for sex on the floor?" she teased. Tormented, too, because while his hands were occupied with carrying her, she kept touching him. Kept driving him crazy. Until he dropped her onto the bed, yanked off his boots and settled on top of her.

Harlan grabbed her jeans and pulled them off. Panties, too. He saw the tiny white scars on her belly and some letters tattooed on her left hip.

She followed his gaze to what had snagged his attention. "I had navel rings. Relics from my wild-child days."

Now all hidden away for him to rediscover. That sent a rush of fire through him, but he stopped when he looked at the letters again.

H. M.

"Harlan McKinney," she provided.

"You had my initials tattooed on your body?" He felt his mouth drop open.

"Hey, a girl's first time is a big deal, and I didn't have enough money to put your whole name there."

He was touched. And sad that she'd obviously thought so much of him.

"No trips down memory lane," she insisted, and kissed him so hard and deep that memory lane vanished.

Harlan kissed her right back. Not just her mouth either. But her breasts again. Her belly. Yeah, the tat. Before he went even lower and kissed her in the hottest, wettest part of her body.

"We didn't do this at Rocky Creek." She made a sound of pleasure and wound one hand into his hair. Her other hand clamped onto the bedding as if she was trying to anchor herself.

"We didn't do a lot of things."

Like go back for seconds, something that Harlan thought he might like to do tonight, especially since it was clear that this wasn't going to last nearly as long as he wanted.

"I want you naked," he heard her say a split second before she gave his hair a yank.

That got him moving up her body again. Caitlyn used her hands and feet to slide off his jeans and boxers, and even with all that moving around and adjusting, she still managed to get in some pretty potent kisses. She also pulled him on top of her.

Exactly where he wanted to be.

But thankfully all his common sense wasn't gone, because he fumbled in the nightstand drawer, located a condom and somehow managed to get the darn thing on even with Caitlyn pulling and tugging at him.

"No virgin surprises this time," he heard her whisper.

But the jolt was still there when he pushed inside her. Pure pleasure. There went his breath again, and he didn't care if he ever got it back. The only thing that mattered now was moving inside her and finding the release for the powder keg of pressure roaring through every inch of him.

Caitlyn was clearly on the same page when it came to pressure and release. She lifted her hips. Dug her fingers into his back. And met him thrust for thrust.

He felt the climax ripple through her body. Saw it, too, in the depths of her crystal-blue eyes. Heard it in her uneven breath. She mumbled something.

His name, he realized.

With his name still shaping her lips, she pulled him down to her. And kissed him.

Harlan returned the kiss. Hard and deep. And with Caitlyn's taste in his mouth, he let her take him to the only place he wanted to go.

CAITLYN WONDERED WHY she was still so wide-awake when she desperately needed sleep. She'd dozed on and off, but that was about it.

Her body was slack from the great sex, and she had a nice little sexual buzz still going on. Plus, she was in Harlan's bed snuggled in his arms while he snoozed away.

It should have been a perfect recipe for sleep.

If she could only turn off her mind.

For the first time in days, it wasn't the investigation that was weighing her down. Nor was it the sex or the anticipation of it. It was the consequences of sex that troubled her now. Harlan would regret it. Not the act itself, but he would likely feel as if he owed her something.

Like dinner.

Or dates.

He knew that she wouldn't expect anything from him. After all, she hadn't so much as whimpered when they'd parted company sixteen years ago.

Well, she hadn't whimpered in front of him anyway.

But she had spent plenty of nights sobbing her eyes out for a boy she thought was so far above her that she would only pull him down into the gutter with her. But now there was no bad-girl gutter, just the massive differences in their chosen careers.

But after sex, even that didn't feel like an obstacle.

And that was why even if Harlan knew he didn't owe her, he would feel as if he did. Because he was a good man to the very core. She'd known that sixteen years ago, and she certainly knew it now.

"Don't you ever stop thinking?" he mumbled.

She looked down at him as he peeked out at her from one partially opened eye. "You can hear me think?"

"Pretty much." He hauled her closer, chest to chest, and tucked her head beneath his chin. "Other than your navel, what else did you have pierced?"

Caitlyn couldn't help it—she smiled. "You don't want to know."

Harlan pulled back, met her gaze. "Now I really want to know."

Mercy, he was even hotter post-sex with that rumpled black hair and sleepy gray bedroom eyes.

"I had my nose pierced." Caitlyn touched the spot that had long since healed. "My eyebrow." Also healed. "And my earlobes." She still had double sets of those, but once there had been a quadruple line of piercings.

He stared at her, obviously waiting. "Nothing else?"

"Sorry to ruin your erotic fantasies."

"Nothing's ruined." He ran his thumb over her bottom lip. "So, what were you thinking so hard about?"

Uh-oh.

Here it came. The dreaded relationship conversation. Caitlyn figured Harlan wasn't any better at this than she was. She also figured it was a conversation he didn't even want to have. She sure didn't.

"I was planning our wedding." And she didn't crack a smile when she said it.

That got his eyes wide-open.

Now she smiled. "Wait. Did I say wedding? I meant our next round of this." She slid her hand between them and touched, touched, touched. "Actually, I was thinking you've gotten really good at sex."

"So have you." Harlan pulled her back to him for a kiss, and just like that she was all hot again.

Sheez.

She wasn't a teenager, but she was acting and feeling like one.

The kissing continued. Not fast and frantic like before. But slow and lazy. Oh, yes. This time there'd be foreplay, and even though she'd just had Harlan, she wanted him and the foreplay all over again.

"Do I owe you an apology? A heart-to-heart talk?" Even with his mouth on hers, she could feel his smile. "Or an engagement ring?"

She smiled, too. "I'll settle for what you're doing right now."

But the last word had barely left her mouth when Harlan's phone buzzed.

He cursed, got up and located his jeans on the floor. Not easy to do, since every item of their clothing was scattered around. Still naked, he took out the phone and jabbed the button to answer it.

Harlan's back was to her, but Caitlyn could see the anger over the interruption drain from his body. He turned and met her gaze, and she saw that the anger had been replaced by serious concern.

"Who?" Harlan snapped. But he obviously didn't get an answer, because he repeated it until he was practically shouting into the phone.

That got Caitlyn moving, and while she tried to hear what was going on, she snatched up her clothes and started dressing. "What happened?" she asked the second Harlan ended the call. He, too, put on his jeans.

"That was Billy. He said someone's kidnapped him. The person dragged him from his car and took him to Rocky Creek."

Her stomach went to her knees. Not only because she

was concerned for Billy but because she knew this meant Harlan had to respond.

"Who did this?" she asked.

But Harlan shook his head and tugged on his boots. "Billy said it was someone wearing a ski mask."

Which told them nothing, because it could be any of their suspects.

Including Billy himself.

"Billy said if I brought anyone else to Rocky Creek, the kidnapper warned him that he'd start shooting." Harlan pressed a button on his phone, sandwiched the cell between his shoulder and ear and kept dressing at a frantic pace. As if every second counted.

And it probably did.

"It could be a trap." But she knew Harlan had no doubt already considered that.

"I'm sure of it, but I have no choice. I have to go."

It was his job, yes, but Caitlyn wanted to grab him and make him stay put.

"Slade," Harlan said when his brother came on the line. "We got a huge problem. Someone's kidnapped Billy. And Declan."

"Declan?" Caitlyn said on a gasp. Oh, God.

"Yeah, Declan," Harlan verified and went back to his phone conversation with Slade. "We have to get out to Rocky Creek right away."

Chapter Fifteen

Everything inside Harlan was racing—the bad thoughts and the fear for his brother's life. But he forced himself to think. He couldn't go off half-cocked when all of this could be a trap. One that could get Caitlyn, Declan, Billy, him and God knew who else killed.

First things first. He tried to call Declan, hanging on to the hope that this was all a hoax, that Declan would answer and assure him that he hadn't been kidnapped.

But the call went straight to voice mail.

Next up, he tried the number Billy had just used to call him. No answer there either.

That got Harlan moving even faster, and he grabbed some extra ammunition from the top shelf of his closet. An extra weapon, too, so he'd have a backup.

"Declan's really been taken?" Caitlyn asked. There was little color in her face now, and her hands were trembling.

"Probably." And Harlan could blame himself for that. "I shouldn't have planted the lie about the fingerprint."

Her shoulders went back. "You had no idea this monster would go after Declan."

No, but he should have anticipated it. He'd counted heavily on the guy trying to destroy the so-called fingerprint evidence. And maybe that was still the plan. The killer could be using Declan as a distraction.

Harlan made another call—this time to Slade. "Make sure you keep someone at the morgue."

Slade assured him that he would, and Harlan quickly ended the call so he could head out. "I'll take you to stay with Kirby and Stella—"

"I can help."

He took her by the arm and got her moving. "You can also get killed. Don't argue, because this isn't up for discussion. You'll stay with Stella, Kirby and Wyatt. The ranch hands will be around, too, and all of them know how to shoot."

"You really think the killer would come here?"

No. He didn't. And that was why Harlan had come up with this plan to leave her here. There were a dozen ranch hands plus Wyatt. The main house had a brand-new security system, something that just about everyone in town was talking about. The killer would know this wasn't the place for a showdown. Besides, killing them wouldn't destroy the evidence.

Unless the killer knew the fingerprint was fake.

That put a hard knot in his gut, but Harlan didn't back down on his plan. He led Caitlyn through his house and to the front door. His truck was parked just on the other side of the fence. Just a few yards away. But he didn't go barreling out into the darkness. He took a few precious seconds to look around. He didn't see anyone lurking in the shadows, but that didn't mean someone wasn't there.

"Wait here," he ordered and hurried out the door.

He braced himself for shots. For anything. But nothing happened, thank God.

Harlan jumped into his truck, started it and backed up enough so he could drive through the fence. The wood pickets went flying, and he stopped directly in front of the steps. He threw open the passenger door.

Even though Caitlyn was visibly shaken, she got moving when he motioned for her to get in. The second she was on the seat, she slammed the door, and he sped away. Toward the main house that was about a quarter of a mile away.

He took out his phone again to call Stella and tell her what was going on, but before he could press in her number, his cell buzzed, and he saw Billy's number on the screen. That didn't help the knot in his stomach. Yeah, he needed to talk to Billy, but he hoped like the devil that the man wasn't about to deliver some bad news.

"The kidnapper gave me a written message to pass on to you," Billy said.

"Who is he, and why the hell doesn't he tell me himself?" Harlan fired back.

"I don't know who he is, but I think he wants me to talk to you so you won't hear his voice. He says you have to bring Caitlyn with you."

Harlan didn't even have to think about it. "No way."

"If you don't, he'll kill Declan."

It was a good thing he'd reached the ranch house and could come to a stop. "Tell the kidnapper to let me talk to Declan," Harlan insisted. Because even though it wasn't something he could accept, he had to know if his brother was still alive. "Now!" he added when he didn't get an immediate response.

There were some sounds of the phone being moved around, and the seconds crawled by. Caitlyn sucked in her breath and scrambled across the seat until her ear was pressed right to his.

"Harlan," he finally heard Declan say.

Relief flooded through him. Fear, too. His brother

was alive, and now he had to figure out how to keep it that way. "What happened?"

"I'm sorry. So sorry." Declan sounded drunk. Or rather drugged. "I was in the parking lot at work and someone hit me with a Taser."

Just as the killer had done to Caitlyn and him. "Are you okay?" And now it was Harlan's turn to hold his breath.

"He gave me something, some kind of drug, and I don't even think I can stand up."

Harlan knew the exact feeling. "Who took you?"

"None of our suspects. This guy's a hired gun, and the person who hired him is staying out of the picture."

Or maybe was elsewhere so he could attack. After all, Declan wasn't the primary target. Now the question was—had the killer used Declan to draw them out to Rocky Creek, or was this some kind of distraction to launch another attack? Or maybe a break-in at the morgue?

"I'll kill him." From the other end of the line, the voice tore through the silence, and it wasn't Declan or Billy. In fact, Harlan didn't think he'd ever heard that voice before.

"Who are you?" Harlan demanded.

"Someone who's going to kill your kid brother if you don't do as I say. And I'll keep killing until Caitlyn and you are out here. You've got forty-five minutes."

His heart dropped. "Not enough time." And Harlan didn't mean just distancewise either. It wasn't enough time for him to think up a way around this.

"Then you'll have to hurry, won't you?" the man taunted. "And remember, don't bring anyone with you or the bullets start flying. Just Caitlyn and you."

"Wait." Harlan tried to think. "It'd be suicide for me

to take Caitlyn in there. What kind of assurance do I have that you won't just kill us all?"

"None," the man readily answered. "But if you don't come, people are going to start dying."

Harlan had no trouble recognizing the next sound. The blast of a gunshot. Even though the sound came through the phone, it was still deafening, and it rocketed through him.

"Declan?" he shouted.

But Harlan was talking to himself, because the line went dead.

CAITLYN HAD TO make Harlan understand what needed to happen here. "There's no way I'll let you sacrifice Declan for me."

Even though her voice was shaking like the rest of her, she left no room for argument. Still, she saw the argument in Harlan's eyes.

"Declan's a lawman." He sounded as if he was trying to convince himself along with her. "I can figure a way out of this."

"And if you show up without me, you could all be dead before you have time to think of it." In fact, someone might already be dead.

That possibility twisted everything inside her.

She tried to reassure herself that the kidnapper wouldn't kill Declan, because he was the bait. The bargaining tool, as well. But it was possible that Billy had been shot or was already dead.

Unless, of course, Billy was behind this.

"We're wasting precious time," Caitlyn reminded him. "Start driving to Rocky Creek."

But he didn't. Harlan sat there, his attention volleying

between her and the ranch house, where he'd intended to leave her.

"Look, we'll work out the details as we drive," she added. "And if by the time we get there you don't think you can make it safe, then you can drop me off at the sheriff's office in Rocky Creek."

That caused him to belt out some really bad profanity, but he threw the truck into gear and started driving. Thank God. Caitlyn certainly wasn't eager to rush to a showdown with this monster who'd made their lives hell, but she couldn't live with herself if she got Declan killed.

Harlan took out his phone and sped down the dark country road away from the ranch. "Slade," he said when his brother answered. "There's been a change of plans. Caitlyn and I are driving to the Rocky Creek Children's Facility."

She couldn't hear Slade's response.

"No, it's probably not a good idea," Harlan added to whatever Slade said, "but if I leave Caitlyn at the ranch, she'll try to follow."

She would, no doubt about it, and it was scary that Harlan knew her so well.

"Keep someone on the morgue," Harlan continued, "but we'll need backup. *Quiet* backup," he amended. "You remember how to get to Rocky Creek from that old ranch road?" He paused. "Good. Take that route and try to come up from behind. I don't know where they're holding Declan, but it's probably either inside the main building or close to it."

He finished that call and immediately made another to Dallas so he could ask about how tight the security was at the ranch. "Just a precaution," Harlan said to her when he no doubt saw the renewed concern in her eyes.

The next call was to his brother Clayton. After Harlan

gave him a quick update, he asked him to do a quiet approach to the facility using the east side of the property. The woods where Sherry's body had been found. Harlan also reminded Clayton that Slade would be nearby, probably so they wouldn't accidentally shoot each other.

There was a lot of potential for things to go wrong.

"What about me? What do you need me to do?" she asked the moment he ended the call with Clayton.

But Harlan didn't answer. He kept driving and punched in another number. This time he put the call on speaker. However, the person who answered didn't say anything either.

"Billy?" Harlan greeted. "Are you there?" Nothing. But Caitlyn thought she could hear someone breathing on the other end of the line. "Billy, I need to talk to the man who kidnapped Declan."

"What the hell do you want?" The man's voice was so loud that Caitlyn jumped before she could stop herself. And it wasn't Billy. It was Declan's kidnapper.

"I need to work out some kind of deal," Harlan said.

"The only deal you're going to get is the one I already gave you. You and Caitlyn need to get out here and come alone. Nothing about that needs to be worked out."

"But it does." Harlan glanced at her, and even though he didn't say anything to her, he shook his head. "Caitlyn's sick, throwing up all over the place. I don't even think she can stand up."

That explained the headshake. He didn't want her jumping to say that she'd be there. Still, Caitlyn doubted the lie would work, especially since this guy likely had plans to kill them.

"She's pregnant," Harlan added. "We started seeing each other a couple of months ago. In secret. I didn't want to tell my family or anyone else because of this Webb investigation hanging over us. Talk to your boss, because I don't think he'd want to put a pregnant woman in the middle of a mess like this."

She figured the guy would just laugh that off, but he stayed quiet for several moments. "I'll get back to you on that."

Harlan punched the end-call button. "If he agrees, you're going to the sheriff's office." He mumbled something she didn't catch. "And if he doesn't agree, then it's probably Farris who's behind this."

Oh, yes. Because a pregnancy would only make Farris want to kill her even more. But if it was Billy, Devin or Curtis, why did they even want Harlan and her?

"Why would the killer want us dead if he still believes there's an incriminating fingerprint on Sherry's body?" she asked.

Harlan shook his head. "I'm not sure how any of this fits. Or if it fits at all. It could be just Farris playing a sick game."

For a moment Caitlyn thought she might indeed throw up. Her stomach was churning. "And if so, then you just made yourself a target, because Farris will think you fathered this make-believe baby. He'll be so enraged that he'll want to tear you apart."

"Hopefully. Anything to make him come after me and not Declan and you."

That turned her blood to ice. No way did she want Harlan to take the brunt of this, but how could she stop it?

How?

Maybe if she had a chance to speak to Farris, she could bargain with him. Maybe even make him believe that she'd go with him if he'd just call off this stupid plan. Of course, she couldn't go with him because he'd likely just kill her the first chance he got. But she might be able to buy them some time so that Harlan could rescue Declan, and maybe even Billy.

Harlan swore and looked at the phone screen as if trying to will the kidnapper to call back. The minutes and miles were just dissolving, and Harlan's mood got worse when the headlights landed on the sign ahead of them.

Rocky Creek Children's Facility.

He took the turn, but he switched off his headlights.

"I want a gun," Caitlyn insisted.

Harlan tipped his head to the glove compartment. "There's one in there."

Caitlyn opened it and pushed aside some plastic handcuffs and papers so she could grab the .38. She prayed she wouldn't have to use it, especially since she wasn't that good a shot. If it came down to her having to take out the killer and the kidnapper, then she and Harlan would be in deeper trouble than they already were.

Harlan pressed the redial button on his phone and again put the call on speaker.

"No deal," the kidnapper said the moment he answered. "You bring Caitlyn here with you."

Thanks to the moonlight, she got a glimpse of Harlan's jaw muscles that had turned to steel. "I want to talk to your boss, and I'm not taking no for an answer."

Harlan took the final turn, and ahead Caitlyn could see the silhouette of the sprawling facility. It looked even more menacing in the dark, and even though she didn't have second thoughts about coming here, Harlan apparently did.

He stopped the truck.

"You'll have to take no for an answer," the kidnapper insisted. "My boss is, well, indisposed right now."

Maybe because he was at the morgue trying to destroy evidence that didn't exist. If so, it was possible that whoever Slade had watching the place would capture him. And if not, that meant someone had to nab this kidnapper and get him to confess the name of the person who'd hired him.

Not exactly an easy night's work.

"Call him," Harlan insisted. "Tell him I'm not bringing Caitlyn unless he speaks to me." With that line drawn in the sand, Harlan hung up.

And the waiting began.

So did Caitlyn's renewed attempts to get Harlan to budge. "Stating the obvious here, but I don't want you to risk Declan's life for me. Besides, Farris won't just kill me once I step from the truck. He'll want...some time with me," Caitlyn settled for saying.

There went her stomach again. Another lurch. Mercy, she didn't want Farris within a hundred miles of her, but using herself as bait was the only way to reason with him.

"And if it's not Farris?" Harlan's question hung in the air, and he turned his head so their gazes met. "This person could want us dead simply because he thinks we've uncovered something that'll incriminate him as Webb's killer."

Yes, she'd considered that, but she could almost feel Farris nearby. It didn't make sense, and she wasn't the sort to rely on gut feelings or intuition, but she couldn't dismiss the feeling that Farris had some part in this.

She checked the time on the dash clock. Time was almost up. Well, it was if they were to believe the kidnapper's ultimatum that they had to arrive within forty-five minutes.

"What happens if he doesn't call back?" she asked.

Harlan opened his mouth to answer, but then he

stopped. His gaze slashed to her side of the truck. Except his attention didn't land on her, but outside the window.

"Get down!" he shouted, and he drew his gun.

He didn't wait for her to move. Harlan caught the back of her neck and shoved her down onto the seat.

Chapter Sixteen

Harlan braced himself for an attack, for bullets to come bashing through the truck. He kept his gun aimed and ready while he pinned Caitlyn beneath him.

But nothing happened.

It was hard to hear over his own pulse pounding in his ears and Caitlyn's ragged breathing, but he damn sure didn't hear any bullets. He lifted his head so he could try to get a better look at the shadowy figure that he'd seen just seconds earlier.

"Stay down." Caitlyn latched on to him and tried to pull him back onto the seat with her.

"I think he's gone," Harlan let her know.

"Who was it?"

He had to shake his head, but it wouldn't have been Slade or Clayton. If they'd somehow managed to get out here ahead of him, they wouldn't be in this area of the grounds. Maybe it hadn't been the kidnapper either, because there was a huge possibility that the killer had hired more than one henchman. God knew how many hired guns Caitlyn and he would have to face, and that was the biggest reason of all for him to throw the truck into gear and haul her butt to the sheriff's office. It had been a huge mistake bringing her here.

"Declan," she reminded him.

He wasn't about to let his kid brother die, but he was pretty sure Declan and he were of a like mind on this. Neither would want to sacrifice Caitlyn to save themselves. Of course, Caitlyn was insisting the same thing about them.

Harlan waited, and the seconds seemed to be flying by. He took out his phone again to call the kidnapper, but he also moved off Caitlyn so he could put the truck in gear. He spared her a glance to see how she was holding up—not well—but then he kept his attention pinned to their surroundings. Hard to do with the moon creating some eerie shadows over the trees and shrubs.

He pushed the redial button. And waited. Waited some more. Until he thought his heart might beat out of his chest. Everything inside him yelled for him to get Caitlyn out of there, so he threw the truck into Reverse. Maybe the kidnapper would see that he was leaving and answer the damn call.

Or not.

Harlan had barely touched his foot to the accelerator when the blast came. He didn't see the shooter, but he felt the impact, all right. The bullet slammed into the front windshield, taking out the safety glass and zinging past his head.

Caitlyn screamed for him to get down, and he did. Harlan also gunned the engine and tried to put some distance between them and the shooter.

More shots came.

Not just one either, but bullets began to pelt the truck. Whoever was shooting at them was almost directly ahead, maybe behind one of the trees that was close to the road.

Since Harlan couldn't lift his head enough to see where he was going, he tried to do the best he could to keep the truck on the road. He also fired a blind shot in the direction of the shooter in the hopes that he'd get lucky. Or at least get the guy to duck behind cover.

It didn't work.

The shots didn't slow down one bit, and it didn't take long before the truck jolted. And Harlan knew why. The gunman had shot out the front tire. Maybe both of them. Harlan lost what little control he had of the steering wheel, and they slammed into the ditch.

With the impact, both Caitlyn and he flew into the dash. His shoulder hit the steering wheel, and by some miracle he managed to hang on to his gun. However, Caitlyn wasn't so lucky. He heard the heavy jolt her body took, and even though she immediately tried to scramble to get her gun, Harlan didn't think it would be easy to find in the darkness and with all hell breaking loose.

More bullets came, and even though he tried to steer the truck, things went from bad to worse when he realized they couldn't move. They'd landed in a ditch filled with several inches of water. Just enough to bog down the tires on the driver's side of the truck.

A bullet crashed through the passenger's window, and even though Caitlyn was still searching for her gun, the sheet of safety glass crashed against her head.

Hell. The shooter had moved, maybe closing in on them from the right. He couldn't just sit there while they were gunned down. The metal exterior of the truck wouldn't keep them safe much longer. Maybe his brothers would arrive soon, hear the shots and give him some backup.

Harlan fired a shot in the direction of the shooter, and in the same motion he threw open his door. Not easy, because he had to push the bottom of the door through the boggy ditch. However, he finally got it open wide enough that he could get Caitlyn out of there.

"This way." He reached across the seat and hauled her closer.

Caitlyn continued to fumble for the gun and grabbed it just before Harlan dragged her out with him. Both of them stepped into the ditch. Definitely not dry. It was filled with stagnant water and clotted mud, and he sank all the way to his knees.

He used the door for cover and kept track of the angle of the bullets. They were still coming from the other side of the truck. Good. Maybe they'd stay that way at least for a few more seconds.

"Move fast," Harlan warned her, and he stepped out of the ditch, pulling her along with him.

He didn't even try to stay on his feet, because it would make them too easy a target. With Caitlyn in tow, Harlan dove behind the nearest tree. They hit the ground hard, and he landed right on the same shoulder that had slammed into the dash. The pain shot through him, but he ignored it and came up ready to fire.

Harlan pulled the trigger, the bullet landing somewhere in the direction of the shooter. He waited to see if the guy would move and come after them.

But nothing.

No more shots.

Harlan drew Caitlyn even closer until he had her pressed against the tree. She, too, had her gun aimed across the road where the shooter had fired his last shot, but all that either of them could do was keep their aim ready and listen for any sound of movement.

Nothing.

Where the devil was this guy?

Harlan glanced up the road at the building. Still no sign of anyone there, not even any vehicles. Not that he'd expected the kidnapper to have Declan in plain sight, but he hoped that his brother wasn't anywhere in the line of fire.

Caitlyn was trembling now, and her breath was gusting to the point that he was worried she might hyperventilate. He didn't want to say anything out loud for fear it would help the shooter pinpoint them, but Harlan did brush his lips on her temple. It wasn't much, but it was the best he could offer for now. Once he got her out of this, though, he'd owe her a huge apology for nearly getting her killed.

That thought had no sooner crossed his mind when he finally heard something. Definitely not a shot.

But footsteps.

Not coming from the front of the truck either, but from the back.

Harlan moved again, pushing Caitlyn behind him so he could face the person making those footsteps. The person wasn't exactly skulking and was coming at them fast. Maybe it was one of his brothers trying to make enough noise so that Harlan wouldn't shoot first.

Even though Harlan couldn't actually see Caitlyn, he felt her adjust, and she moved her gun into position, too. They waited, breaths held.

They didn't have to wait long.

The person came out from the back of the truck. Running. Harlan couldn't make out who the guy was before he launched himself at Caitlyn and him.

BEFORE CAITLYN COULD get out of the way, the man plowed into them, knocking Harlan, her and himself to the ground. Once again she lost the grip on the gun and it went flying. Too bad she couldn't have flown with it, because both men crashed right down onto her.

Suddenly she was fighting for her breath. She couldn't

move, but mercy, she could feel. She felt as if she'd been hit by a couple of Mack trucks.

Harlan latched on to the guy and shoved both himself and the man off her. Thank God. Still fighting for breath, Caitlyn rolled to the side and tried to pick through the darkness to see who'd done this. She seriously doubted it was Clayton or Slade, because they probably would have said something before launching an attack.

And there was no doubt about it—this was an attack.

The man threw a punch at Harlan, and it connected, but it glanced right off his jaw as if he hadn't even felt it. Maybe because the blow hadn't been that hard, but also because Harlan had to be operating on pure adrenaline.

Caitlyn certainly was.

Despite the crushing pain in her chest, she groped around on the ground, searching for the gun she'd dropped. Harlan might need her as backup if something went wrong with this fight.

A shot blasted through the air.

Sending her heart to her knees.

Despite the other shots, the sound was still unexpected, and deafening. And it robbed her of her breath again.

"Harlan?" she shouted. But she couldn't tell if he'd been hit or if he'd even been the one to fire that shot.

The scuffle continued with fists flying and with the men tangled around each other in the fight. They stumbled backward and would have crashed into her again if Caitlyn hadn't scrambled out of the way just in the nick of time.

Harlan's back bashed into the tree. She heard the sound of pain he made. His profanity, too. And despite that pain he came up fighting. He drew back his gun and knocked the guy upside the head.

Still the man didn't stop.

Caitlyn saw the weapon he had clutched in his hand. He made a feral sound. More animal than human. And though she didn't recognize his voice, there was something about that sound, some raw emotion in it that she did recognize.

"Farris?" she called out.

The man stopped. For just a fraction of a second. And he turned toward her as if he were trying to launch himself at her.

Harlan didn't let that happen.

He grabbed Farris by the throat and slung him to the ground. Unlike her, however, Farris held on to his gun, and even though he was on the ground, he pointed the weapon directly at her.

Caitlyn froze.

"Marshal, if you pull the trigger, I'll pull mine," Farris warned. "And Caitlyn will die."

God. This was exactly what she'd spent months trying to avoid. Yes, Harlan was armed, and he had his gun pointed at Farris, but Farris could get off a shot, kill her and then turn that gun on Harlan.

She had to do something to stop this.

"You have no reason to kill Harlan." She tried to keep her voice level. Hard to do, since she was shaking from head to toe.

"Yeah, I do." Farris was shaking, too, and she prayed he didn't pull that trigger before she could talk him out of it. "I know you're pregnant, and I know it's his kid."

She shook her head. "No. I'm not pregnant."

"You're lying. I heard Harlan when he said it, and he was practically gloating."

So Farris had been listening in on that call. No surprise there, since it was his hired gun they'd been talking to. The person had likely kidnapped Declan and Billy, too, because Farris wouldn't have wanted to get his hands dirty like that.

But he'd saved his fight to come after her.

"How could you have gone to his bed?" Farris spat out the words, and without taking his eyes or gun off her, he got to his feet. Less than a yard away from Harlan.

"I didn't," she lied. She shook her head when Harlan inched closer to Farris. Probably because he was planning to knock that gun from his hand.

Or try.

But Caitlyn was hoping it wouldn't come to that.

"Harlan hates me," Caitlyn said, "because I'm writing an article about his foster father. I'm spilling all the details of how the marshals are covering up his involvement in Jonah Webb's murder."

Farris glanced at Harlan. Maybe to see if he could tell if that was true. Harlan didn't jump to defend her, thank God, but there must have been something about Harlan's expression that made Farris's mouth twist into a snarl.

"Don't you know that I see you've been with him?" Farris fired back.

Yeah, she could see that, and she could argue it until she was blue in the face, but Farris wasn't going to believe her. It was time to go with plan two.

"I'll go with you," she told Farris.

Now Harlan protested. First with some vicious profanity. And while he didn't exactly look at her, she could feel every muscle in his body reacting to that. "You're not going anywhere with this nutcase."

"That's not your decision to make," Farris fired back. Though he still didn't sound convinced that she was telling the truth.

And she wasn't.

No way would she leave with him. Heaven knew what kind of sick ways he could come up with to torture her before he killed her. And he would kill her. His obsession and rage wouldn't allow him to keep her alive. But Caitlyn was counting heavily on Harlan being able to stop a getaway. All she needed to do was give Farris enough distraction for Harlan to get the jump on him.

She took a step closer to Farris, hoping that it was distraction enough.

It snagged Farris's attention, all right. His split-second glances turned just slightly longer each time his gaze swung in her direction. He was obviously trying to figure out if he could trust her. Or at least trying to figure out how to get her out of there while neutralizing Harlan.

"I'll go with him," she said to Harlan.

Like Farris, Harlan gave her only a quick glance, but in that simple glance something passed between them. She saw his silent assurance that he was not going to let her die.

Too bad that Farris must have seen it, too.

A strangled groan tore from Farris's throat. "You're in love with him. You bitch!"

And that was the only warning she got before Farris launched himself at her. He didn't reach her.

Thanks to Harlan.

Before Farris could get to her, Harlan tackled him, and again both men crashed to the ground. This time, though, she saw Farris's gun go flying, and Caitlyn knew this fight was pretty much over. Harlan not only outsized him, he'd been trained how to fight.

Still, Farris fought like a wildcat, all the while yelling and flailing his arms around. One punch from Harlan, however, and Farris's head flopped back.

Caitlyn reached for Farris's gun so that he wouldn't

be able to snatch it up, but reaching for it was as far as she got.

Someone hooked an arm around her neck, and her body snapped back. She landed right against his chest. And before she could make a sound, someone shoved a gun to her head.

Chapter Seventeen

Harlan had to restrain himself, but part of him wished that Farris was dead so the man could no longer torment Caitlyn.

But he wasn't about to murder an unarmed man.

Especially one he could restrain. He grabbed Farris and hauled him to his feet so he could drag him to the truck and get a pair of plastic handcuffs from the glove compartment.

Harlan stopped when he caught a movement from the corner of his eye, and without loosening his grip on Farris, he whirled in Caitlyn's direction.

Everything inside him came crashing down.

No, hell, no. This couldn't be happening. But it was. Caitlyn was standing there, white as a ghost in the pale moonlight, and someone had a gun on her.

"I didn't see him in time," she whispered.

That felt like a fist around his heart. She was apologizing for being put in another life-and-death situation. One not of her own making. It was Farris's making.

Or maybe not.

Harlan had to amend that theory when he caught a glimpse of the man's face. Not some hired gun. He knew this man.

Curtis.

"You said I could have Caitlyn," Farris practically shouted. "You said you wouldn't hurt her."

"There's been a change of plans." Curtis's voice was eerily calm, and unlike Farris, his hand wasn't shaking.

The mark of a cold-blooded killer.

"Marshal McKinney, you need to put down your gun and step away from Farris," Curtis ordered.

Harlan didn't budge, but Farris struggled, fighting to get away from him. However, Harlan held on. He didn't want Farris going after Caitlyn. Not with that gun right at her head. Even if Curtis didn't have plans to shoot her, the gun might accidentally go off.

"This guy isn't dealing with a full deck," Harlan said, tipping his head to Farris. "If I let him go, he might try to kill all of us."

"He won't." And there didn't appear to be a shred of doubt in Curtis's tone, which meant they'd worked out some kind of sick deal.

Caitlyn didn't say a word. Didn't take her gaze off Harlan, and he cursed when he realized that she was still giving him an apologetic look.

"Your gun," Curtis reminded Harlan. "And let go of Farris so he can leave."

Farris made another of those outraged sounds. "I'm not leaving without her." Again he tried to tear himself away from Harlan, but Curtis shifted the gun toward Harlan and him.

"My advice—cooperate." And coming from Curtis, it didn't sound like a suggestion. "If things work out as planned, you might be able to have Caitlyn after all." Curtis's mouth tightened. "Though why you'd want a woman in love with another man, I don't know."

It was twice in one night that someone had accused her of being in love with him, and if Harlan hadn't been between this rock and a hard place, he might have given it some thought. However, the only thoughts he had right now were how to get out of this.

Caitlyn muttered something and shifted her body weight as if she might drop to the ground. Curtis hooked his arm around her neck, snapped her to him and pointed the gun at her again.

As bad as it was to see that gun right on her—and it was bad—Harlan had to look at the bigger picture here. He had to keep Curtis's mind off the fact that Harlan was still armed. The longer he could hang on to his gun, the better.

"Where's Declan?" Harlan wanted to know the answer to that, but he wasn't sure he'd get the truth from Curtis. Still, the conversation might distract him until Harlan could figure out a way to get that gun from his hand.

"He'll join us soon. At gunpoint, of course."

Harlan didn't doubt the gunpoint part. In fact, there might be several hired guns in on this. But why was he bringing Declan here?

"You plan to use Declan for more leverage?" Harlan asked. But he already had the ultimate leverage with Caitlyn.

"You don't need Declan or Harlan down here if you have me," Caitlyn volunteered. "You can let them go."

Curtis made a sound of disagreement. "I need you both, actually. You and Harlan," he clarified, aiming a glare at Farris. "Temporarily. Just hold on to your sanity a moment or two longer, and you might get what you want from this."

Because Harlan still had a grip on Farris, he felt the man's muscle tense. "I paid big money to get her," Farris shouted. "Hell, I funded this entire operation for one reason. *Her.*"

So that explained, well, pretty much nothing. Farris had the money to pay for an attack like this, but Harlan still didn't know the reason Curtis would plan their capture and murder.

But he could guess why.

"It's your fingerprint they'll find on Sherry's neck," Harlan challenged.

Curtis didn't jump to deny it. "There'll be no fingerprint to find, because right about now someone's blowing up the morgue."

Harlan had no idea if that was true, but at that exact moment his phone buzzed. He couldn't take his attention off Curtis to see who was calling and why. But maybe if someone had tried to set an explosive at the morgue, then the person watching the place had managed to stop it.

He could hope anyway.

Curtis obviously hoped the opposite because he smiled. For a moment or two anyway. Then he glanced down at his watch and cursed.

Was this profanity for Declan because he hadn't arrived yet? Or was something else going on? Either way, Harlan hoped he had his own backup in the area. Certainly by now Slade and/or Clayton should be nearby, and he hoped like the devil it didn't take them too long to get here.

"This is the third time I've asked you to put down that gun," Curtis warned Harlan. "If I have to ask again, I start shooting, and Caitlyn will get the first bullet."

Now Harlan cursed. Because he knew time for distraction was over. He couldn't risk Caitlyn's life, so he dropped his gun on the ground. Right by his feet. Maybe he'd be able to get to it in a hurry if things turned bad.

And he was afraid *bad* was just getting started.

"You murdered Sherry," Caitlyn concluded, obviously trying to make her own distraction. "And now you're trying to cover it up by using us." Despite the gun at her head, she tossed Curtis a glare. "Did you kill Tiffany, too?"

"I had to. I'd already killed Sherry and needed a way to cover it up." Curtis lifted his shoulder. "I figured if the Rangers would try to link Tiffany's death to Webb's murder, then they'd try to link Sherry's, too."

"And you wanted Sherry dead because she was asking questions about some of your shady business investments." Plain and simple, it was a guess, but judging from the way Curtis's eyes narrowed, Harlan had hit pay dirt. "So you sent out those threatening notes to make everyone believe her disappearance was connected to Rocky Creek."

"I sent those notes," Farris piped up.

Curtis huffed as if dealing with an annoying insect. "Because I told him to do it. Farris isn't much of a self-starter when it comes to detailed plans like this one. All that psychosis gets in the way."

Taunting a crazy man wasn't how Harlan would have gone about this. However, it was obvious Curtis wasn't pleased with the man who'd paid to cover up a murder, all so he could get his hands on Caitlyn.

"I'm guessing that Curtis promised he'd draw out Caitlyn for you," Harlan asked Farris.

"He promised more than that," Farris confirmed. "He contacted me out of the blue and said he could draw her out. He told me I could do whatever I wanted and that I wouldn't have to go back to that place."

To the institution, no doubt.

Curtis checked his watch again. Cursed some more.

The man was obviously unaware or just didn't care that Farris was about to snap.

"Henry?" Curtis called out. Probably to the man who'd kidnapped Declan.

No answer.

And that only made Curtis's profanity even worse.

"You think Curtis will keep his promise to you?" Caitlyn asked, her attention nailed to Farris now. "You really believe he'll let you out of this alive? Not a chance. No way would he let a loon like you go so you could spill to every lawman in the state."

Farris stopped struggling, his gaze locked with Caitlyn's. Hell. She was baiting him. The very thing Harlan didn't want her to do, even if she was trying to get Farris to go after Curtis and not her.

"Don't listen to her," Curtis snapped.

"He doesn't want you to listen because he knows I'll tell you that you've been duped. All that money you spent, and he has no intention of following through on his promises." She paused, managed a syrupy smile. "Because he intends to keep me for himself."

Farris froze. Unlike Caitlyn, Harlan couldn't see the man's expression, but he didn't need to see it to feel the rage roar through Farris's body.

Before Harlan could stop him, Farris ripped out of Harlan's grip and, screaming, lunged for Caitlyn.

Just as a shot blasted the night air.

THE SHOT CAME so close to Caitlyn's right ear that she felt the heat from the bullet. And the deafening noise. God, it was awful. The pain stabbed through her head, and she would have fallen to her knees if Curtis hadn't kept a death grip choke hold around her neck.

But Farris was the one who dropped to his knees.

With his gaze frozen on her, he slipped to the ground. "I'll always love you," Farris said.

Even though the pain made everything sound like a roar, she somehow managed to hear the words. Sickening words from a sick man.

Farris reached out as if he might try to touch her, but Curtis kicked at him, his boot connecting with Farris's hand. Grunting in pain, Farris pulled back his hand and clutched it to his chest.

Where the bullet had slammed into him.

"Goodbye, Caitlyn," Farris mumbled, and he slumped into a heap.

Caitlyn didn't have to feel his pulse to know he was dead. She could see it on his now lifeless face. There was no way she could feel sorry for him. Not after everything he'd done, but she was also painfully aware that the biggest threat wasn't Farris.

But rather Curtis.

Now that he'd killed Farris and confessed to Sherry's murder, there was no way he'd let them walk out of there alive. Of course, there was no way she and Harlan would just stand by while he shot them either. But Curtis was the one with the gun.

There was a rustling sound to her left, and while keeping her firmly in his grip, Curtis pivoted in that direction. Harlan moved, too. Toward his gun on the ground next to Farris.

"If you pick it up, she dies," Curtis warned him.

Harlan stopped, but the rustling sound didn't.

"Henry?" Curtis called out.

"Not Henry," the person answered.

Slade.

Caitlyn felt instant relief followed by instant fear. Slade sounded close. Very close. And that meant he could be hurt. It was bad enough that she and Harlan were in danger—Declan, too—but she didn't want to add any more of Harlan's family members to the mix.

"Who are you?" Curtis demanded.

"Marshal Slade Becker. And I'm guessing you're about to be dead."

That didn't help with her fear. Yes, Slade was likely a good shot, but Curtis's gun was still pressed right to her head. Worse, at any second he could turn that gun on Harlan.

Curtis dragged her toward a tree until his back was right up against it. That would make it much harder for Slade to get off a shot.

And that meant this was likely a standoff.

"Where's Declan?" Harlan called out to his brother. He didn't take his attention off her, and his body was in a position as if he was primed and ready for a fight.

"Safe and with Clayton. He's a little groggy from being drugged, but he'll be okay. We've cuffed the kidnapper."

Caitlyn had no idea if that was true, but prayed it was, because it meant Curtis had no backup.

Curtis reacted to what Slade had said by cursing and digging the gun barrel into the side of her head. She felt the skin break and the sting of pain. Felt the warm blood, too.

But the worst was seeing Harlan's reaction.

Anger seemed to jolt through his entire body, and she shook her head, praying he wouldn't do anything that would get him killed.

"They found a guy at the morgue, and he had a bag of explosives with him," Slade continued, his voice calm as if discussing the weather. "I'm guessing so he could blow up the place with Sherry's body inside. The sheriff called in a SWAT team and they have him surrounded."

"Shut up!" Curtis yelled. He cursed and shoved her forward. "Caitlyn's coming with me, and you'll both back off because if you don't, she dies."

This couldn't play out in her favor. Either Harlan would get shot trying to stop Curtis, or if Curtis did manage to take her, she wouldn't live long. She, Harlan and now Slade were the ultimate loose ends.

Maybe even Declan, too.

She had to do something to stop this from becoming worse than it already was. But what? Hard to do much of anything when she didn't have a weapon and Curtis was bigger and stronger than she was.

"I'll go with him." She kept her gaze pinned to Harlan when she said that and hoped he would get out of the way when Curtis started shooting.

And he *would* shoot.

Maybe in the next second or two. He was probably counting on the shots to draw out Slade, since Harlan's brother wouldn't be able to return fire as long as she was Curtis's human shield.

"I'm going to hold you to that dinner date," Caitlyn added.

She saw surprise flash through Harlan's eyes, and she also felt Curtis move the gun away from her head.

Mercy.

He was taking aim at Harlan.

Harlan reacted, already moving down and to the side. Or rather trying to do that so he could scoop up his gun. But she knew there wasn't enough time, because Curtis already had him in his sights.

Caitlyn screamed at the top of her lungs and twisted her body so that she could shove her side against Curtis. It didn't knock him down, but it did cause his hand to move at the exact moment that he pulled the trigger.

The bullet flew past Harlan and smacked into the tree next to him.

Harlan didn't waste any time, and he didn't stoop to pick up his gun. He came right at them, looking very much like a linebacker going after an opposing player. Caitlyn tried to grab Curtis's hand to stop him from firing again.

But she failed.

Curtis pulled the trigger not once but twice, both shots blasting so close to her ear that it drowned out all other sounds. Including whatever Harlan said to her. While he ran toward them, she saw his mouth moving, almost as if he were speaking in slow motion, but she couldn't make out a word.

But she sure felt the impact of Harlan tackling Curtis.

Harlan was a big man, and all those solid muscles plowed right into them. All three went to the ground so hard that Caitlyn could have sworn she saw stars. The pain would have been well worth it.

If Curtis hadn't managed to get off another shot.

Caitlyn couldn't see where the bullet landed, but she prayed it hadn't hit Harlan.

She rammed her elbow into Curtis's stomach and felt the small victory when he yelped in pain. But her victory was short-lived, because he fired again.

And then he bashed the gun against the side of her head.

It was as if her brain exploded, and Caitlyn had no choice but to quit fighting. The only thing she could do was try to get out of the mix so she'd have a better chance of grabbing that gun from Curtis.

She twisted and turned. Tried to maneuver her body

to the side. But she was pinned between them, and she caught the blows coming from both men's fists. It was obvious that Harlan was trying to fight around her, but Curtis kept shoving her right at Harlan's fist.

Caitlyn felt a hard jolt, and for a moment she thought she'd been punched again. But this was no punch. Someone took her by the shoulder, his grip hard and bruising, and he yanked her from the middle of the fight. She caught a glimpse of Slade's face before he slung her on the ground behind him and went after Curtis.

Not that Harlan needed his help.

With her out of the way, Harlan clamped on to Curtis's right wrist and slammed his hand against the tree. The gun finally went flying. But before it even fell, Harlan landed a crushing blow to Curtis's jaw. His head flopped back and his body went limp.

Caitlyn's vision was still blurred from the punches she'd taken. Her hearing sucked, too, because of the bullets fired so close to her ear. But she could see and hear enough to know that this fight was over. Farris was dead and Harlan hauled Curtis to his feet and bashed him into the tree.

Slade pulled a pair of plastic cuffs from his pocket and used them to restrain the man.

"I'll transport him in my vehicle and call the sheriff to see if they have the situation at the morgue contained," Slade volunteered. He looked back at her. "You okay?"

"Fine," she lied. She tried to get up, but her legs were just too wobbly. Caitlyn decided to sit there for a few seconds and catch her breath.

The danger had passed, yes, but it would take a lifetime or two to forget how close they'd all come to dying tonight.

"You should probably run her by the hospital," Slade suggested to Harlan.

Harlan's gaze snapped to her, and she could have sworn the color drained from his face. She must have looked pretty bad for him to have that reaction, and he hurried to help her to her feet.

"Were you shot?" But he didn't wait for her to answer. He shoved her hair from her face and looked her over.

"Not shot," she assured him. However, her panic soon mimicked his when she saw the blood trickling down the side of his head. "Were you?"

He shook his head, snapped her to him and hugged her. It was a little too hard, considering that every part of her was hurting, but Caitlyn didn't pull away. That hug was exactly what she needed.

"This isn't over," Curtis snarled. The look he gave them all could have frozen Hades.

"Sure looks like it's over to me," Harlan snarled right back.

Slade grabbed Curtis and got him moving.

"If you arrest me, he dies," Curtis shouted over his shoulder.

That stopped Slade in his tracks, and he turned and stared at the man. "What the hell does that mean?"

Harlan moved closer, and because he still had her in his grip, Caitlyn got her legs working so she could move, too. This was probably some last-ditch ploy from Curtis to get them to release him, but Caitlyn was positive that wasn't going to happen. Curtis had killed at least two people and had attempted to kill them. The only place he was going was to jail.

But still Curtis smiled.

Definitely not the expression she'd expected, and an icy chill went through her that was bone deep.

"I have an insurance policy." Curtis's smile widened. "If you arrest me, he dies."

No. That icy chill got significantly worse. "Who dies?" Caitlyn managed to ask.

"Kirby, of course. Must have forgotten to mention that I sent a hired gun to the ranch." Curtis met Harlan's stare head-on. "And if he doesn't get a call from me in the next few minutes, his orders are to start shooting."

Chapter Eighteen

Harlan couldn't get his body to move fast enough. He whipped out his phone and punched in the number of the ranch office. The chief hand, Cutter, should have answered the landline, but it rang several times before the answering machine kicked in.

Hell.

He tried Wyatt's cell next because his brother was supposed to be inside the ranch house with Kirby and Stella. But again it rang only once and then went to voice mail.

There could have been a dozen reasons for Wyatt and Cutter not to answer, but Harlan could think of only one very bad one.

The ranch was under attack. His family could need immediate help, and here he was a good forty-five minutes out.

"I'll phone Sheriff Geary," Slade volunteered. He kept a firm grip on Curtis and made the call so he could get some backup out to the ranch. Still, it would take the sheriff at least twenty minutes to arrive.

"My hired gun will be mighty hard to see in the dark," Curtis bragged. "No telling how many places he could hide on a ranch and wait to ambush any- and everyone. You can get all the lawmen you know out there on foot, and it won't save Kirby because you can't kill what you can't see."

It took every ounce of Harlan's restraint not to knock this guy's teeth down his throat. "Call off your man," Harlan demanded.

"Not a chance." Any sign of gloating disappeared, and the eyes of a killer stared back at Harlan. "If I have to rot in a jail cell, then it'll help knowing that you've lost someone you love."

That did it. Harlan caught Curtis's shoulder and bashed him into a tree. "Call off your man," he repeated, and to get his point across he gave Curtis another hard knock.

Curtis laughed. "You think I can file charges for brutality? Heck, might even get the case thrown out because you beat a confession out of me."

Not a chance, and while he would like to add more bruises and maybe a broken bone or two to Curtis's injuries, it was clear this conversation was getting them nowhere fast.

"The sheriff's on his way out to the ranch," Slade relayed to Harlan. "He'll try to contact Wyatt and the others, too."

It was a good start, but not nearly good enough. Harlan needed a vehicle, and unfortunately his truck was literally in a bog.

"What about a chopper?" Caitlyn asked. "Do the marshals have one?"

Harlan shook his head. "The nearest one is in San Antonio, and the sheriff doesn't have one either." They were looking at an hour, maybe longer because it would take an approval higher than Saul to get a chopper in the air.

Kirby, Stella and God knew who else could be dead by then.

Caitlyn snapped her fingers, took his phone and started punching in numbers. "I'm calling my old boss" was all she said.

Harlan wasn't sure she'd get anywhere with this call, but one thing good came out of it. For the first time since his arrest, Curtis actually looked concerned that his plan might not work.

"No time to explain," Caitlyn said the moment her boss answered. She was talking so fast that her words ran together. "But you know all those favors you owe me— well, I'm cashing in. I need the news chopper in the air *now*. Get it out to the Blue Creek Ranch near Maverick Springs." She paused. "Yes, that's the place. Put on the search-and-find lights. There's a gunman on the loose out there, and people are in danger."

Harlan hadn't realized he was holding his breath until she hit the end-call button and handed him back his phone. "He's on the way out there."

Good. Though a reporter probably wouldn't have a way to take out the gunman, at least the lights might help pinpoint the guy's location.

"My truck's that way, parked just up the road," Slade said, tipping his head in that direction and tossing Harlan his keys. "Take Caitlyn with you and leave now. Clayton, Declan and I will take this piece of slime and catch up with you."

Harlan didn't refuse his brother's offer, and even though Caitlyn didn't appear to be in any shape to run, he didn't want to leave her alone there with Farris's body. And he damn sure didn't want her having to ride back to Maverick Springs with the man who'd just tried to murder her.

"Curtis could be lying," Caitlyn said when he caught her hand and got them moving.

Yeah. And Harlan had to remind himself that a lone hired gun would be seriously outnumbered by Wyatt and the other ranch hands. Plus, the security system would have alerted them that they had an intruder trying to break into the house.

Well, unless Curtis had somehow managed to take that out, too.

But Harlan didn't allow himself to go there. He just ran, and when it was clear that Caitlyn wasn't going to be able to keep up with him, he scooped her up in his arms and ran as fast as he could.

His lungs were burning when he finally reached Slade's truck, and he practically shoved Caitlyn inside. She clearly had injuries on her face and arms, and he prayed he wasn't making things worse with his rough treatment.

"Give me your phone," she insisted. "I'll keep calling while you drive." But she didn't wait for him to hand her the phone—she yanked it from his pocket.

"Try Dallas first. His number should be in there because I called him earlier." He started the engine and drove out of there fast.

Thank God there was no traffic at this hour. No rain or fog either. Of course, he'd be driving like a crazy man, so that created more than enough obstacles in their path.

Every passing second seemed to take hours, and with each of those seconds, his worries skyrocketed. Even if Caitlyn and he got there before the gunman could start shooting, that would only put her right back in danger. He couldn't do that to her, but he had to help his family.

Caitlyn scrolled through the recently called numbers, located Dallas's and pressed the button. Harlan heard the call go to voice mail. His nerves were already shot, and that sure didn't help.

"Who should I try next?" she asked.

Harlan mentally went through the possibilities. "Try the house's landline," he finally said, and he rattled off the number.

He heard the rings from the other end of the line. And he prayed and waited. He stopped counting at five rings and was ready to tell her to hang up and call someone else. But then Harlan heard a voice.

Stella.

"Who's there?" Stella demanded.

Caitlyn hit the button to put the call on speaker. "It's me, Harlan. What's going on?"

"Maybe some trouble," the woman immediately answered. Her voice was a whisper. "Somebody set off that new security alarm, and Cutter, Dallas and Wyatt are out there trying to figure who it is."

So unless this was a horrible coincidence, Curtis hadn't been bluffing. He had indeed sent someone. Even though he was already speeding, Harlan went even faster, and prayed the miles would disappear between him and the ranch.

"It's a gunman hired by Curtis Newell," Harlan told her, "and he has orders to shoot up the place."

"Great day in the morning." Stella also mumbled something he didn't catch. "I doubt Wyatt and the others will answer their phones. Probably got the ringers off. What should I do, Harlan? It's dark out there, and trying to find a gunman would be like looking for a needle in a haystack."

Yeah, and the guy could just hide until he had an easy kill shot. "A helicopter's on the way. It might help. In the meantime stay down and stay quiet. Kirby, too," Harlan added. "I don't want either of you taking any chances."

"But if someone could get hurt—"

"Wyatt and Dallas know how to handle this," he said, cutting off any protest. No way did he want Stella out there facing down a hired killer. "Sheriff Geary should be out there any minute now. Call him and tell him what's going on so he doesn't walk into an ambush."

"I will, but get here as fast as you can."

Oh, he would do that. He damn sure didn't want Curtis claiming any more victims. It was bad enough that he'd gotten his hands on Caitlyn.

Harlan glanced at her, but it took more than several glances to take it all in, and what he saw turned his stomach. Even in the thin moonlight, he could see the blood. Not just one spot either but multiple places, including a line running from her eyebrow to her chin.

He'd lost count of how many punches she'd taken while in the middle of his fight with Curtis. Too many, that was for sure.

Harlan cursed, shook his head. "Look what that SOB did to you."

"That bad, huh?" She leaned over and looked in the rearview mirror. "Yeah, that bad."

Caitlyn used the back of her hand to swipe at the blood. Since there was blood on her hand, that didn't work very well, so she grabbed some tissues from his glove compartment. But she didn't dab at her face. She dabbed at his, and even though Harlan tried not to react, he winced when she hit a sore spot.

"Look what that SOB did to you," she repeated.

Harlan didn't want to do a mirror check, but he could

feel some of his injuries. Maybe even a cracked rib or two. Still, he'd gotten off lucky.

Because Caitlyn was alive.

The realization of that miracle hit him so hard that he hooked his arm around her and pulled her closer to him. He needed to feel her next to him. Needed to know that she was somehow going to forgive him for not doing a better job of protecting her.

"I'm sorry." He kept his eyes on the road, but he brushed a very gentle kiss on her injured cheek.

She pulled back, looked at him. "For what?"

"For not living up to that complete-package notion you had about me."

That earned him a scowl. "I would give you an elbow jab for that, but I don't want to add to the bruises." She settled against him as if that was exactly where she belonged. "You lived up to the *notion* just fine."

Harlan kept his attention fastened on the road, but he couldn't push the other thoughts out of his head. Thoughts of Caitlyn. Not just of all the bad things that had gone wrong since she'd come back into his life. But of the things that had gone right, too.

Like this moment with her next to him. Making love to her. Hell, just being with her.

"Look." Her head whipped up from his shoulder, and she pointed to the night sky.

Even with just a quick glance, Harlan saw the light in the distance. The helicopter had arrived and had a giant spotlight aimed at the ranch.

He hadn't thought it possible, but time seemed to go even slower, and he could have sworn it took him an hour to drive those last two miles. However, the closer he got, the brighter the light was from the helicopter.

Harlan flew past his place and drove the last leg to

the main house. When he took the final curve, he saw someone. And not just someone but a man holding a rifle. His heart went to his knees until he realized that someone was Wyatt.

And he wasn't alone.

Dallas and Cutter were there. The sheriff, too, and they all had weapons pointed at a man kneeling on the ground.

Harlan slammed on the brakes and jumped out. Caitlyn did, too, and she hurried to his side. Just in case things weren't as under control as he thought, Harlan stepped in front of her.

"You're a little late," Wyatt greeted him. "Thanks to the chopper, we found this moron about two minutes ago. Don't worry. Everyone's okay. He didn't get off a shot."

The relief was instant. A lot of prayers had been answered tonight. "You can thank Caitlyn for the chopper," Harlan let his brother know.

"Well, thank you, darlin'." It was Wyatt's usual charming tone, and he aimed that rock-star grin at Caitlyn. A grin that dissolved right away when his gaze landed on them.

"Sheez, you two look like hell," Wyatt mumbled at the same time Dallas said, "How many fights did you lose tonight?" Dallas didn't wait for an answer, because his phone buzzed.

"We won the important one," Harlan insisted.

Well, the important one against Curtis anyway. Harlan figured there was another battle he had left to fight, and this one was just as important as life and death. He put his arm around Caitlyn and pulled her closer to him.

"I'll get this guy into town," the sheriff volunteered.

"I want a plea deal," the man grumbled as Sheriff Geary led him to the cruiser parked just a few yards away. "I'll tell you whatever you want to know. I've got proof that Sherry found out Curtis was laundering money. I stashed away some emails and notes. I'll give 'em to you for a plea deal."

"The only way that deal will happen is if you also have proof that Curtis killed her," Harlan argued.

"Got that, too. He killed her himself. Strangled her right there in her office and then he had me help him cram the body into a freezer at my hunting cabin. I'll show you where it all happened if I get that plea deal."

Harlan wasn't about to refuse the information, but it wouldn't be needed to convict Curtis. Not only did they have his confession, he'd murdered Farris in front of them.

"Clayton, Slade and Declan are on their way to the jail with Curtis," Dallas relayed when he ended his call. "And I just let the chopper crew know the threat was over so they could leave."

Good. One less thing to worry about. Next on his list was getting Caitlyn checked out by the doctor. Well, the next to the next thing. He had something he had to get off his mind first, and it wouldn't wait.

"I don't want just a dinner date with you," Harlan told her.

Caitlyn blinked, and thanks to the chopper he had no trouble seeing her surprised expression. He braced himself for some comeback that would dismiss everything they'd found together.

She shook her head. "And I don't want just sex with you."

Dallas cleared his throat and muttered something about needing to check on Kirby and Stella. Wyatt mumbled something about them finding a bed—soon.

Harlan ignored them both and kissed her. He tried

to keep it gentle because they were cut in all the wrong places, but he wanted it to be hot and deep enough to cloud her head a little. Or maybe just to make her remember that they had something special here.

The sheriff's cruiser drove past them. The chopper turned and whirled away, taking the clopping noise with it. But Harlan didn't break the kiss until breathing became an issue.

He pulled back, gathered his breath so he could say what he needed to say.

"I'm in love with you."

Except he wasn't the one to say it. Caitlyn did. She took the words right out of his mouth.

"Run for cover if you feel the need," she continued. "But I've been in love with you since I was sixteen. And though I'm sure you'd like me to feel differently, I'm still in love with you."

He smiled. Winced. Smiled again. "I want you in love with me because I'm in love with you."

Now she smiled. Slow and easy. She grabbed a handful of his shirt and snapped him to her. Yeah, they both winced, but Harlan was sure the heat and love overpowered the pain.

"Marry me," he said. Harlan made sure it wasn't exactly a question. Because he couldn't take no for an answer.

Caitlyn had been in his life for a long time, and now he wanted her in his heart for even longer.

For a lifetime.

She nodded. "Yes, and if I could say it any faster, I would, because I don't want you to change your mind."

He had no intention of changing his mind and showed her with another kiss.

"Caitlyn, you'll always be my first," he said with his lips touching hers. "And my last."

She smiled. "Even better." Caitlyn kissed him to show him how much she meant it.

* * * * *

COMING NEXT MONTH from Harlequin® Intrigue®
AVAILABLE JULY 23, 2013

#1437 SHARPSHOOTER
Shadow Agents
Cynthia Eden
Sydney Sloan is ready to put her past behind her—only, her past isn't staying dead. She doesn't know if she can trust sexy ex-SEAL sniper Gunner Ortez...or if he is the man she should fear the most.

#1438 SMOKY RIDGE CURSE
Bitterwood P.D.
Paula Graves
When Delilah Hammond's former lover, injured FBI agent Adam Brand, mysteriously lands on her doorstep, she risks everything to help him catch a criminal who'll stop at nothing to destroy Adam's reputation.

#1439 TAKING AIM
Covert Cowboys, Inc.
Elle James
Tortured former FBI agent Zachary Adams must battle his own demons while helping a beautiful trail guide rescue her FBI sister from a dangerous drug cartel.

#1440 RUTHLESS
Corcoran Team
HelenKay Dimon
Paxton Weeks's newest assignment is to keep a close eye on Kelsey Moore. But when Kelsey's brother is kidnapped, Pax is forced to add bodyguard to his list of duties....

#1441 THE ACCUSED
Mystere Parish: Family Inheritance
Jana DeLeon
Alaina LeBeau thought returning to her childhood home would help her reconnect with lost memories, but someone doesn't want her to remember. And the gorgeous town sheriff, Carter Trahan, is determined to find out why.

#1442 FALCON'S RUN
Copper Canyon
Aimée Thurlo
Relentless and hard-edged, Detective Preston Bowman knew that helping ranch owner Abby Langdon solve a murder depended on keeping his emotions in check—but destiny had yet to have its say.

You can find more information on upcoming Harlequin® titles, free excerpts and more at www.Harlequin.com.

HICNM0713

REQUEST YOUR FREE BOOKS!
2 FREE NOVELS PLUS 2 FREE GIFTS!

HARLEQUIN

INTRIGUE

BREATHTAKING ROMANTIC SUSPENSE

YES! Please send me 2 FREE Harlequin Intrigue® novels and my 2 FREE gifts (gifts are worth about $10). After receiving them, if I don't wish to receive any more books, I can return the shipping statement marked "cancel." If I don't cancel, I will receive 6 brand-new novels every month and be billed just $4.74 per book in the U.S. or $5.24 per book in Canada. That's a savings of at least 14% off the cover price! It's quite a bargain! Shipping and handling is just 50¢ per book in the U.S. and 75¢ per book in Canada.* I understand that accepting the 2 free books and gifts places me under no obligation to buy anything. I can always return a shipment and cancel at any time. Even if I never buy another book, the two free books and gifts are mine to keep forever.

182/382 HDN F42N

Name	(PLEASE PRINT)

Address	Apt. #

City	State/Prov.	Zip/Postal Code

Signature (if under 18, a parent or guardian must sign)

Mail to the **Harlequin® Reader Service:**
IN U.S.A.: P.O. Box 1867, Buffalo, NY 14240-1867
IN CANADA: P.O. Box 609, Fort Erie, Ontario L2A 5X3
**Are you a subscriber to Harlequin Intrigue books
and want to receive the larger-print edition?
Call 1-800-873-8635 or visit www.ReaderService.com.**

* Terms and prices subject to change without notice. Prices do not include applicable taxes. Sales tax applicable in N.Y. Canadian residents will be charged applicable taxes. Offer not valid in Quebec. This offer is limited to one order per household. Not valid for current subscribers to Harlequin Intrigue books. All orders subject to credit approval. Credit or debit balances in a customer's account(s) may be offset by any other outstanding balance owed by or to the customer. Please allow 4 to 6 weeks for delivery. Offer available while quantities last.

Your Privacy—The Harlequin® Reader Service is committed to protecting your privacy. Our Privacy Policy is available online at www.ReaderService.com or upon request from the Harlequin Reader Service.

We make a portion of our mailing list available to reputable third parties that offer products we believe may interest you. If you prefer that we not exchange your name with third parties, or if you wish to clarify or modify your communication preferences, please visit us at www.ReaderService.com/consumerschoice or write to us at Harlequin Reader Service Preference Service, P.O. Box 9062, Buffalo, NY 14269. Include your complete name and address.

HI13R

*When Jacie Kosart's twin sister needs rescuing from a
dangerous drug cartel, she turns to tortured former FBI
agent Zachary Adams. But can Zach put aside his own
demons to help a beautiful damsel in distress?*

Zach staggered back. The force with which the woman hit
him knocked him back several steps before he could get
his balance. He wrapped his arm around her automatically,
steadying her as her knees buckled and she slipped toward
the floor.

"Please, help me," she sobbed.

"What's wrong?" He scooped her into his arms and carried
her through the open French doors into his bedroom and laid
her on the bed.

Boots clattered on the wooden slats of the porch, and more
came running down the hallway. Two of Hank's security
guards burst into Zach's room through the French doors at the
same time Hank entered from the hallway.

The security guards stood with guns drawn, their black-clad
bodies looking more like ninjas than billionaire bodyguards.

"It's okay, I have everything under control," Zach said.
Though he doubted seriously he had anything under control.

He had no idea who this woman was or what she'd meant by
help me.

Hank burst through the bedroom door, his face drawn in
tense lines. "What's going on? I heard the sound of an engine
outside and shouting coming from this side of the house."
He glanced at Zach's bed and the woman stirring against the
comforter. "What do we have here?"

She pushed to a sitting position and blinked up at Zach.
"Where am I?"

"You're on the Raging Bull Ranch."

"Oh, dear God." She pushed to the edge of the bed and
tried to stand. "I have to get back. They have her. Oh, sweet
Jesus, they have Tracie."

Zach slipped an arm around her waist and pulled her to him
to keep her from falling flat on her face again. "Where do you
have to get back to? And who's Tracie?"

"Tracie's my twin. We were leading a hunting party on the
Big Elk. They shot, she fell, now they have her." The woman
grabbed Zach's shirt with both fists. "You have to help her."

"You're not making sense. Slow down, take a deep breath
and start over."

"We don't have time!" The woman pushed away from
Zach and raced for the French doors. "We have to get back
before they kill her." She stumbled over a throw rug and hit
the hardwood floor on her knees. "I shouldn't have left her."
She buried her face in her hands and sobbed.

Zach stared at the woman, a flash of memory anchoring his
feet to the floor.